D1012731

Dear Reader,

If you thought there were no more Oz books after the original fourteen by L. Frank Baum, do we have a marvelous treat in store for you. Ruth Plumly Thompson, named the new Royal Historian of Oz after Baum's death, continued the series for nineteen volumes. And we will be reviving these wonderful books, which have been out of print and unattainable anywhere for almost twenty years.

Readers who are familiar with these books swear that they are just as much fun as the originals. Thompson brought to Oz an extra spice of charming humor and an added richness of imagination. Her whimsical use of language and deftness of characterization make her books a joy to read—for adults and children alike.

If this is your first journey into Oz, let us welcome you to one of the most beloved fantasy worlds ever created. And once you cross the borders, beware—you may never want to leave.

Happy Reading,
Judy-Lynn and Lester del Rey

THE WONDERFUL OZ BOOKS
Now Published by Del Rey Books

By L. Frank Baum

By Ruth Plumly Thompson

*Forthcoming

Grampa in
OZ

by
Ruth Plumly Thompson

Founded on and continuing the Famous Oz Stories

by
L. Frank Baum

"Royal Historian of Oz"

with illustrations by
John R. Neill

A Del Rey Book
Ballantine Books • New York

Cover design by Georgia Morrissey
Cover illustration by Michael Herring
Text design by Gene Siegel

Library of Congress Catalog Card Number: 84-91221

ISBN: 0-345-31587-1

This edition published by arrangement with Contemporary Books,
Inc.

Manufactured in The United States of America

First Ballantine Books Trade Edition: June 1985

10 9 8 7 6 5 4 3 2 1

This book is dedicated, with deep affection, to Uncle Billy
(Major William J. Hammer)
Author, inventor and second cousin to Santa Claus

—Ruth Plumly Thompson

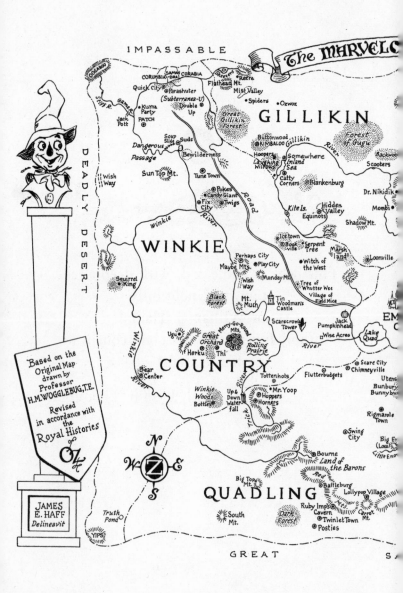

IMPASSABLE

The MARVELO

COGDANO

CORUMBIA SAMAN-DRA CORABIA
Quick City
Parashuter
(Subterranea-U)
Double
Up

Reera
Flathead Mt.
Mist Valley
Spiders
Ozwoz

GILLIKIN

Game
Kuma
Party
PATCH
Jack
Pott

Soap
Slide Suds
Dangerous
Passage
Bewilderness

Sun Top Mt.

Tune Town

Wish
Way

Pokes
Candy Giant
Fix
City
Twigs

Great
Gillikin
Forest

Buttonwood
KiMBALOO Gillikin
Hoopers
Laughing
Willows
Catty
Corners

Somewhere
Inland
Sea
Blankenburg

Forest
of Gugu

Backwoo
Scooters

Dr. Nikidik

Mombi

Kite Is.
Equinots

Hidden
Valley

Shadow Mt.

WINKIE

Winkie
River

Squirrel
King

Perhaps City
Maybe Mts.
Play City

Wish
Way

Black
Forest
Mt.
Much

Monday Mt.

Ice town
Bool
ville
Serpent
Tree

Marsh
land

Loonville

Witch of
the West

Tree of
Whutter Wee
Village
of Field Mice

Tin
Woodman's
Castle

EM

COUNTRY

Ugu

Great
Orchard
Herku Thi

Merry-Go-Round
Mts.

Rolling
Prairie

Scarecrows
Tower

Jack
Pumpkinhead
Wise Acres

Lake
Quad

Winkie
River

Bear
Center

Winkie
Wood
Bottles

Up &
Down
Water
fall

Tottenhots

Mr. Yoop
Hoppers
Horners

Flutterbudgets

Scare City
Chimneyville

Utens
Bunbury
Bunnybu

Rigmarole
Town

Swing
City

Big En
(Long)
Little Eno

Bourne
Land of
the Barons

QUADLING

Big Top
Mt.

South
Mt.

Truth
Pond

YIPS

Red
Baffleburg

Dark
Forest

Ruby Imps
Cavern
Twinlet Town
Posties

Lollypop Village

Carrot
Mt.

GREAT

SA

Based on the
Original Map
drawn by
Professor
H.M.WOGGLEBUG,T.E.

Revised
in accordance with
the
Royal Histories
of
OZ

JAMES
E. HAFF
Delineavit

DEADLY DESERT

Griff R.

N
W E
S

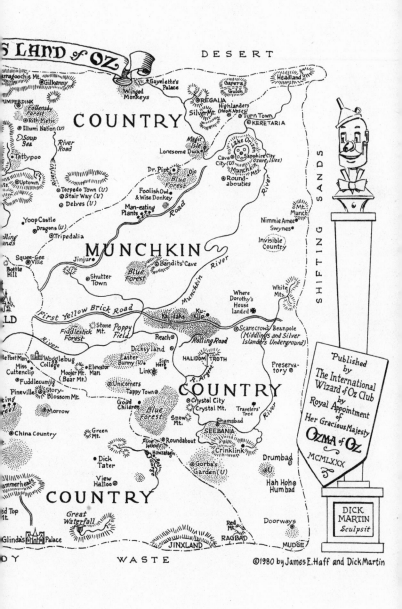

S LAND of OZ

DESERT

SHIFTING SANDS

COUNTRY

Tamagoochie Mt.
Gilkenny
UMPERDINK
Follensby Forest
Rith Metic
Illumi Nation (U)
Soup Sea
Tattypoo
Uptown
River Road
River (U)
Torpedo Town (U)
Stair Way (U)
Delves (U)
Yoop Castle
Dragons (U)
Tripedalia
olling ands
Squee-Gee Ville
Bottle Hill
Jinjur
Shutter Town
Blue Forest

Winged Monkeys
Gayelette's Palace
Gapers Gulch
Headland
REGALIA
Silver Mt.
Highlanders (Hook Noses)
Turn Town
KERETARIA
Magic Isle
Lonesome Duck
Dr. Pipt
Ojo
Blue Forest
Foolish Owl & Wise Donkey
Man-eating Plants
Road
Cave
City (U)
Sapphire City
Ozure Isles
Munchkin Mts.
Round-aboutes
Mt. Munch
Nimmie Amee
Swynes
Invisible Country
Bandits' Cave

MUNCHKIN

Munchkin River

Where Dorothy's House landed
White Mts.
Kalidah
Ku-Klip
First Yellow Brick Road
Stone Mt.
Fiddlestick Forest
Poppy Field
Reach
River
Dicksyland
Easter Bunny (U)
Sign Here
Link
Scarecrows Beanpole
(Middlings and Silver Islanders Underground)
Rolling Road
HALIDOM
TROTH
Preservatory
 he Post Man
Miss Cuttenclip
Wogglebug College
Moojer Mt. (Bear Mt.)
Elevator Man
Fuddlecumjig
Pineville
Story-Blossom Mt.
Morrow
Unicorners
Tappy Town
Good Children
Blue Forest
Crystal City
Crystal Mt.
Snow Mt.
Shamsbad
SEEBANIA
Travelers' Tree
R. Argent
R. Argent River

COUNTRY

China Country
Green Mt.
Dick Tater
View Halloo
Pine Woods
Bowzatap
Roundabout
Crinklink
Gorba's Garden (U)
Drumbad
U
Hah Hohe Humbad

COUNTRY

ammerhead
ed Top Mt.
Glinda's Palace
Great Waterfall
JINXLAND
Red Mt.
RAGBAD
Doorways
MUDGE

DY

WASTE

©1980 by James E. Haff and Dick Martin

Published by The International Wizard of Oz Club by Royal Appointment of Her Gracious Majesty **OZMA of OZ** MCMLXXX

DICK MARTIN Sculpsit

Grampa was an old Soldier who had fought in Nine Hundred and Eighty Battles

List of Chapters

CHAPTER 1

A Rainy Day in Ragbad

KING FUMBO of Ragbad shook in his carpet slippers. He had removed his red shoes, so he could not very well shake in them.

"My dear," quavered the King, flattening his nose against the cracked pane, "will you just look out of this window and tell me what you see?"

"*My Dear*" was really the Queen of Ragbad and years ago, when she had first come to the old red castle on the hill, she had worn her crown every day and was always addressed as

1

"Your Majesty!" But as time passed and affairs in the kingdom had gone from bad to worse, *My Dear*, like many another Queen, had taken off her crown, put on her thimble and become plain Mrs Sew-and-Sew, and with all her sewing she had barely been able to keep the kingdom from falling to pieces. She was stitching a patch on the King's Thursday cloak at this very minute I am telling you about.

"What now!" gasped the poor lady, and rushing to the window she also pressed her nose to the pane.

"Do you see what I see?" choked King Fumbo, clutching at her hand.

"I see a great cloud rolling over Red Mountain," panted Mrs Sew-and-Sew. "I see the red geese flying before the wind. I see—" Here she gave a great bounce and brushed past her husband— "I see my best patch work quilt blowing down the highway!" moaned Mrs Sew-and-Sew, stumbling across the room.

"Ruination!" spluttered the King as the door slammed after his wife. "Shut the bells! Ring the windows; fetch Prince Tatters and call my red umbrella! Grampa! Scroggles! Where is every Ragbad-body?"

Grampa, as it happened, was in the garden and Grampa was an old soldier with a game leg who had fought in nine hundred and eighty Ragbad battles and beaten everything, including the drum. Just now he was beating the carpet. Tatters, the young Prince of Ragbad, was off

2

on a picnic with the Redsmith, and Scroggles, the footman-of-all-work about the castle, was mending a hole in the roof, so none of them heard the King's calls.

Finally, seeing that no one was coming to carry out his commands, Fumbo began to carry them out himself. First he clutched his red beard and jumped clear out of his carpet slippers. Next he slammed the window on his thumb. With his thumb in his mouth he hurled himself upon the bell rope, pulling it so violently the cord broke and dropped him upon his back. Having failed to ring the bell, he wrung his hands—and well he might, for the room had grown dark as pitch and the wind was howling down the chimney like a pack of hungry gollywockers.

"I'll get my umbrella," muttered King Fumbo, scrambling to his feet, but just as he reached the door, ten thousand pounds of thunder clapped the castle on the back and so startled poor Fumbo that he fell through the door and all the way down ten flights of steps. And worse still, when he finally did pick himself up, instead of running into the throne room, he plunged out into the garden and the storm broke right over his head—broke with such flashing of lightning and crashing of thunder, and lashing of tree tops, that the King and such other luckless Ragbadians as were out were flung flat on their noses, and the ones who were indoors crept under beds and into cup-

3

boards and wished they had been better than they had been. Even Grampa—who was far and away the bravest man in the country—even Grampa, after one look at the sky, rolled himself in the carpet he had been beating and lay trembling like a tobacco leaf.

"This will certainly spoil the rag crop," sighed Grampa dismally, and as he spoke right out in this frank fashion of the chief industry of Rabgad, I'd better tell you a bit more about the country itself, for I can see your nose curling with curiosity and curly noses are not nearly so becoming as they used to be.

To begin with, Ragbad is in OZ—a small patch of a kingdom way down in the south-western corner of the Quadling country. In the reign of Fumbo's father it had been famous for its chintz and tapis trees, its red ginghams and calico vines, its cotton fields and its fine linens and lawns. Indeed, at one time, all the dress goods in Oz had been grown in the gardens of Ragbad.

But when Fumbo came to the throne, he began to spend so much time reading and so much money for books and tobacco that he soon emptied the treasury and had no money to pay the chintz and gingham pickers, nor to send the lawns to the laundry—they were always slightly dusty from being trodden on—and one after another the workers of Ragbad had been forced to seek a living in other lands, so that now there were only twenty-seven families left, and the cotton fields and calico bushes, the chintz and tapis trees, from lack of care and cultivation, ran perfectly wild and yielded—instead of fine bolts of material—nothing but shreds, tatters and rags.

The twenty-seven remaining Ragbadians, including the Redsmith, the Miller, the Baker and twenty-four rustic laborers, after a vain attempt to do the work of twenty-seven hundred, gave up in despair and became common ragpickers. From these rags, which fortunately were still plentiful, Mrs Sew-and-Sew and the good wives of Ragbad made all the clothing worn in the kingdom, besides countless rag rugs, and the money obtained from the sale of these rugs was all that kept the little country from absolute and utter ruin.

Of the splendid courtiers and servitors surrounding Fumbo's father only three remained, for I regret to say that neither the servants nor the old nobility had been able to stand the hardships attendant upon poverty, and they had left in a body the first morning Mrs Sew-and-Sew had served oatmeal without cream for breakfast. The army, too, had deserted and marched off to Jinxland because the King could not buy them new uniforms, so that only three retainers were left in the old red castle on the hill. Pudge, the oldest and fattest of the wise men, had stayed because he was fond of his room in the tower and of Mrs Sew-and-Sew's coffee. Scroggles, the second footman, had stayed because he had old-fashioned notions of his duty, and Grampa, though long since discharged from active service, had stuck to his post like the gallant old soldier he was, and as there were no battles to fight, he tended the furnace, weeded the gardens and helped King Fumbo and Mrs Sew-and-Sew bring up their son to as fine a young Prince as any in Oz.

It was of Prince Tatters—during all this bluster—that Grampa was thinking as he lay shivering under the carpet, and as soon as the thunder stopped hammering in his ears he stuck out his head. The wind, after snatching off ten roofs, the wings from the red mill and shaking all the little cottages till their very chimneys chattered, had rushed away over Red Mountain. It was still raining, but Grampa, seeing that the worst was over, crawled out of the carpet and began to look for trouble. And what do you s'pose he found? Why, the King, or at least, the best part of the King!

"Ragamercy!" shrieked the old soldier, jumping behind a tapis tree, a thing he had never done in all of those nine hundred and eighty battles. But his conduct does not surprise me at all, for Fumbo had lost his head in the storm, and was running wildly around without it—stumbling over bushes and vines and stamping his stockinged feet in a perfect frenzy of fright and fury. Now, of course, you will say at once that Fumbo is not the first King to lose

6

his head and I can only answer that he is the first I ever heard of who went on living without it, and if Ragbad were not in the wonderful land of Oz I should say at once that the thing was impossible. In Oz, however, one may come apart, but no one ever dies; so here was poor Fumbo, with his head clean off, as live and lively as ever.

Breathing hard Grampa peered around the tapis tree again to see whether his eyes had deceived him. But no, it was the King, without a doubt, and without his head. "Whatever will

Mrs Sew-and-Sew do now," groaned Grampa, and pulling his campaign hat well down over his ears he dashed out and seizing Fumbo's arm began splashing through the garden, dragging the King along after him. Mrs Sew-

and-Sew had already reached the castle and was sitting on the broken-springed sofa that served for a throne, sneezing violently. She had not only rescued her quilt, but she had caught a frightful cold. All the colors in the quilt had run together, and this last calamity so upset the poor lady that she began sobbing and sneezing by turns. But right in the middle of the fifteenth sneeze, she looked up and saw the old soldier with the game leg standing in the doorway.

"Now don't be frightened," begged Grampa, advancing stiffly and dripping water all over the rug. "Don't be alarmed, but at the same time prepare yourself for a blow."

Mrs Sew-and-Sew, with her damp kerchief in her hand, had already been preparing herself for a blow, but now, dropping the handkerchief, she sneezed instead and when, glancing over Grampa's shoulder she caught sight of the King, she sneezed again and fainted dead away and rolled under the sofa.

"This is worse than a battle," puffed Grampa, dashing between the King and the Queen, for every time he tried to help Mrs Sew-and-Sew the King fell over a chair or upset a table.

"Halt! About face and wheel to your left, can't you?" roared the old soldier, mopping his forehead. But to these instructions Fumbo, having no face about him, paid no attention. Instead he wheeled to the right and swept all the ornaments from the mantel down on the

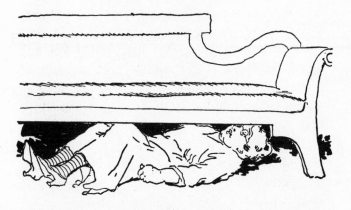

old soldier's head, and then jumped on Grampa's good foot so hard that Grampa forgot for a moment he was a King, and thumped him in the ribs. Then, muttering apologies, the old soldier seized a curtain cord and tied Fumbo to a red pillar. This done, he reached under the sofa, pulled out Mrs Sew-and-Sew, and having nothing else handy gave her a huge pinch of snuff. Just as she came to, in from the garden, splashing water in every direction, rushed Prince Tatters and in from the kitchen pelted Pudge, the aged Wise Man.

"The rag crop is ruined and the King will lose his head!" panted Pudge, who had a bad habit of predicting events after they had occurred.

"Has lost his head," corrected Grampa, jerking his thumb over his shoulder.

"But Grampa!" Stumbling across the room, Prince Tatters shook the old soldier by the arm. "When—how—why—what will he do?"

9

"Do without it," sighed the old soldier, glancing uneasily at Fumbo.

"The King has lost his head, long live his body!" wheezed Pudge, rolling up his eyes.

"Now don't cry, my dear!" begged Grampa, scowling reprovingly at Pudge and patting Mrs Sew-and-Sew on the shoulder. "Having no head really saves one no end of trouble. No face to wash! No more headaches, no ear aches, no tooth aches!" Grampa's voice grew more and more cheerful. "No lectures to listen to, no spectacles to hunt, no hair to lose, no more colds to catch in it. Why he is really better off without a head!"

But Mrs Sew-and-Sew refused to be comforted and rocking to and fro moaned, "What shall we do! What shall we do? What shall we do?"

A Rainy Day in Ragbad

"I tell you," proposed Pudge, pursing up his lips importantly. "Let's all have a strong cup of coffee." As this seemed a sensible suggestion they all filed into the big red kitchen of the castle, leaving Fumbo kicking his heels against the stone pillar.

CHAPTER 2

The Wise Man Speaks

" I SUPPOSE," sighed the old soldier, stirring his coffee with the handle of his sword, "it would do no good to hunt for the King's head in the garden?"

Drying out before the blazing fire in the kitchen stove and sipping Mrs Sew-and-Sew's fragrant coffee the little company had grown more calm.

"I'll just have a look," said Prince Tatters, pushing back his chair, but the old Wise Man shook an impatient finger at the very idea of such a thing.

"When a King's head goes off it goes off," declared Pudge huskily—"Way off as far off as it can go."

"How far is that?" asked the old soldier. "And—"

"Hush, I am thinking," wheezed Pudge, ruffling up his hair with one hand and holding out his coffee cup with the other. "I am thinking and presently I shall speak. Another cup of coffee, ma'am!" This was his seventh cup and after he had sipped it deliberately, scraped all the sugar out of the bottom and licked the spoon, he set down both cup and saucer, flung up his hands and spoke. "Let Prince Tatters go in search of his father's head," said the old Wise Man of Ragbad. "Let him seek at the same time his fortune, or a Princess with a fortune, for otherwise he will end as a common rag-picker."

"But suppose," objected Grampa, who tho' an old bachelor himself had romantic ideas about marriage, "suppose he cannot love a Princess with a fortune. Suppose—"

"It is not wisdom to suppose!" sniffed Pudge. "Hush! I am thinking and presently I shall speak again." He closed his eyes and pressed his fingers to his forehead and after a short silence, during which Mrs Sew-and-Sew took a quick swallow of coffee and Grampa a hasty pinch of snuff, he spoke again. "It is the rainy

13

day," announced Pudge in his most solemn voice, "the rainy day I have long predicted. As the King has lost his head we must ourselves see what he has saved up for it. Come!"

Marching to the King's best bed chamber, Pudge flung open the cupboard and there beside Fumbo's worn cloak hung the only thing he had saved up for a rainy day—a huge red umbrella.

"And must Tatters go out into Oz with only this to protect him from danger?" wailed Mrs Sew-and-Sew, beginning to sneeze again.

"No!" declared Grampa, stamping his good foot. "I myself will accompany him!"

"Oh, Grampa!" cried the Prince, who was too young to realize the dangers of head hunting or the hardship of fortune finding, "may we start at once?"

"Hush!" mumbled Pudge, holding up his finger, "I am thinking." Blowing out his cheeks, he stood perfectly quiet for about as long as it would take to count ten.

"To-morrow morning will be the time to start," said the old Wise Man. "Let us return to the King." Sobering a bit at the thought of his unfortunate father, Prince Tatters followed them down stairs, but every now and then he gave a little hop, for the idea of setting out upon such an adventure thrilled him tremendously. When they reached the throne room, Fumbo was leaning quietly against the post. He had evidently become more used to the loss of his head and was busily twiddling his thumbs.

"If we could just get him a false head till we find his own," sighed Grampa, thumping the King affectionately on the back, "he would look more natural. Ah, I have it!" Plunging out into the wet garden, the old soldier plucked a huge cabbage and hurrying back set it upon the King's shoulders. But no sooner had he done so than Fumbo broke the cord tying him to the pillar, rushed to the kitchen and tried to climb into the soup pot! Indeed, Mrs Sew-and-Sew snatched off his cabbage head just in time to save him from this further calamity.

Panting a little from the exertion and surprise they all sat down to think again. But by this time the news had spread into the village, and the twenty-four rustic laborers, the Miller, and the Baker and the Redsmith came hurrying to the castle to offer their services. They were subjects to be proud of, let me tell you, though a little odd looking in their patched and many colored garments. They listened in respectful silence while Grampa told all he knew of the strange plight of King Fumbo.

"I will make the King an iron head," volunteered the Redsmith eagerly. He had a forge next to the mill and did all the iron work in Ragbad.

"No, no!" protested Grampa. "Iron is too hard. Do you want Mrs Sew-and-Sew to break her knuckles?" he finished indignantly, then dodged behind a pillar, because it was not generally known that Mrs Sew-and-Sew boxed the King's ears every morning.

"I will make the King a new bun—er—head," puffed the Baker, stepping forward importantly, "a head as good as his own!"

"You mean a doughnut?" asked Grampa in astonishment. "Why, that would be splendid!" Fortunately no one heard him this time and as Mrs Sew-and-Sew was pleased with the idea the Baker hurried into the kitchen and with several raisins, some flour, spices, milk and butter, kneaded up and baked a head that was the image of Fumbo's own. It had melancholy prune eyes, red icing for hair and cinnamon whiskers. Once it had been glued on the King's shoulders everyone drew a deep sigh of relief and Fumbo himself walked calmly to his throne and sat down. Promising to bake new heads as they were needed, the Baker said good-night, and as it was growing late the others said good-night too and marched back to the village to repair the damage done by the storm.

But in the castle itself, there was little sleep that night. King Fumbo never closed his prune eyes, for the Baker had given him no eyelids. Prince Tatters, though packed off early to bed, could do nothing but twist and turn and think of the wonderful adventures he would have seeking his fortune. Mrs Sew-and-Sew sat up till the morning star rose over Red Mountain, mending and piecing the few poor garments the Prince possessed, and thinking up good advice to give him with his breakfast.

Grampa, too, had much to occupy him, oiling his gun, packing his knapsack and polishing his sword and game leg. Many old soldiers do

17

a lot of talking about game legs, but Grampa had the real genuine article. It buckled on at the knee and was an oblong red and white ivory box that opened out like a checker board when one wanted to play. Jointed neatly on the end of this was another red box that Grampa used for a foot, and that contained the little red figures one used for playing. The game itself was known as scrum and was a great favorite in Ragbad, being a bit like checkers, a bit like parchesi and a bit like chess.

Grampa was very proud of his game leg, for it not only served him in place of the one he had lost in battle, but whiled away many dull hours, and being hollow was a splendid place to store his pipe and tobacco. The old soldier had seventy-five pipes and deciding which of these to carry with him took longer than all his other preparations. At last even this important matter was settled and he lay down to snatch a few hours' sleep before morning. And morning came in almost no time, the sun rising so bright and cheerily that even Mrs Sew-and-Sew took heart, and when Grampa stuck his head in the kitchen door to see how breakfast was coming she told him how she intended to refurnish the entire castle when he returned with the King's head and the fortune.

"Fine!" cried the old soldier, who was in excellent spirits himself. "And if you will just sew a button on this shirt I'll be ready to start at once!" So while Grampa went on with the

breakfast Mrs Sew-and-Sew, who was frightfully clever with her needle, sewed a button on the shirt. That was all Grampa needed to complete his outfit, so he hurried up stairs to waken the Prince, and at eight o'clock precisely the old soldier and Tatters issued forth from the palace gates.

Grampa wore the red uniform of the Ragbad Guards, with its scarlet coat and checkered trousers and carried not only his knapsack, gun and sword, but his trusty drum as well. Prince Tatters, over his many colored rag suit, had flung the shaggy skin of a thread bear, and with the big umbrella grasped firmly in one hand and a box of lunch in the other, presented so brave and determined an appearance that the twenty-seven good men of Ragbad, drawn up to bid them farewell, burst into loud cheers.

19

The children waved their hats and handkerchiefs and strewed the path of the two heroes with the bunches of posies and ragweed they had risen at dawn to gather. Mrs Sew-and-Sew and the King stood on the balcony waving their arms—she waving both hers and his—for poor Fumbo, with his dough head, had no way of knowing what the excitement was all about and stood there without so much as blinking a prune.

"Good-bye!" choked Mrs Sew-and-Sew, steadying Fumbo with one hand and fluttering her apron with the other. "Don't forget your father's head!"

"Good-bye!" shouted Pudge, leaning far out of his window in the tower to wave his red night cap. Pudge never rose till ten.

Grampa touched his cap, Prince Tatters

waved his umbrella, and having taken the patched flag of Ragbad from Scroggles, who had accompanied them thus far, they wheeled sharply to the left and marched down the broad red highway that led straight out into other and dangerous lands of Oz!

CHAPTER 3

The Blue Forest of Oz

"GRAMPA," said Prince Tatters, after the two adventurers had marched along for a time in silence, "Pudge did not tell us where to look for my father's head, nor where to find the Princess and the fortune."

"Trust a wise man for that," replied the old soldier, striking a match on his game leg and lighting his pipe.

"Then where are we going Grampa?" asked the Prince, shifting his umbrella to his other arm and adjusting his stride to that of the old soldier.

"That," puffed Grampa, "depends on the four-pence." Stopping short, he took a small coin from his pocket. On one side was the head of King Fumbo and on the other the coat of arms of Ragbad. "I may not be a wise man," explained Grampa, tossing the coin in his palm, "but I am sure your father's head can only be restored by magic. There are but two people left in Oz who are permitted to practice magic. One is Glinda, the good sorceress and Queen of our own Quadling country and the other is the Wizard of Oz, who lives in the palace of Princess Ozma, ruler of all Oz."

Tatters nodded impatiently, for he had learned all this in his history book.

"So," continued Grampa, "we must march either to the East—for Glinda's castle is in that direction—or to the North to the Emerald City and the palace of Ozma of Oz. Which shall it be? Heads for Ozma, arms for Glinda!"

Up flew the four-pence and Prince Tatters, dropping on his knee, gave a little cry of delight—for Fumbo's head was uppermost.

"The King has decided himself," chuckled Grampa, pocketing the coin, "so North we go to the Emerald City. We'll be on our way, my lad, and who knows but on the way we may pick up a fortune or a Princess—and a couple of new pipes and some rare old Oz tobacco," finished the old soldier, half closing his eyes. These last two items did not interest Prince Tatters, but the thought of visiting the Capitol of Oz, of seeing Princess Ozma, the little fairy ruler, and being presented at court, sent the Prince, who had spent his whole life in the shabby little kingdom of Ragbad, marching along the red highway so fast that Grampa had to do double time to keep up with him.

Tatters began rehearsing all Mrs Sew-and-Sew had taught him of court manners and speech and wondering whether he had better speak to Grampa about his bad habits. The old soldier had but two. One was eating with his sword and the other was taking snuff, but after a sidelong glance at Grampa, trudging happily at his side, the Prince decided to wait until they reached the Emerald City before offering any advice on etiquette. Even Tatters did not realize how long a journey this would be. He knew in a general way that Oz is a great oblong kingdom, divided into four large countries and many small ones, and that the Emerald City is in the exact center.

On the maps of Oz in the Prince's geography the southern Quadling country was marked in red; the country of the West, which was settled by the Munchkins, was marked in blue; the northern Gilliken country in purple; and the land of the Winkies, which lay to the East, was colored yellow—for these were the national colors of the countries represented.

Though Grampa and Tatters had by this time left Ragbad far behind them, they were still in the Quadling country and all the little farms and villages they passed were of cheery red brick or stone and the people themselves dressed in the quaint red costume of the south. Tulips, poppies and red roses nodded over the tall hedges; the fields, rusty with sorrel, had a red-dish tinge and all along the highway giant red maples arched their lacy branches. At noon they stopped under one of these maples and had a bite of the lunch Mrs Sew-and-Sew had prepared for them, but their pause was short for both were anxious to reach the Emerald City as soon as possible, to learn from the Wizard of Oz the best way to recover Fumbo's head. To make the marching easier, the old soldier played a lively rat-tat upon his drum, and as they passed through the quiet Quadling villages many heads were popped out the windows to see what all the racket was about. But soon these villages became farther and farther apart, and the country more wild and unsettled and just as the sun slipped down behind the tree-tops they came to the edge of a deep blue forest.

"A long march," puffed the old soldier, mopping his forehead, "but we're getting along, my lad, for this is the beginning of the Munchkin country."

"Do you think it's safe?" asked Prince Tatters, peering anxiously into the gloomy forest.

"Safe!" cried Grampa scornfully. "Well I hope not. Fortunes are never found in safe places my boy. Shouldn't wonder if there were a bear behind every tree," he continued cheerfully. "Shouldn't wonder if there were a dragon or two lying in wait for us. Come on!" Thrusting his drum sticks through his belt and waving his sword, the old soldier plunged recklessly into the blue forest, shouting the national air of Ragbad at the top of his lungs.

"Oh, hush," begged Prince Tatters, glancing uneasily from side to side and treading close upon Grampa's heels, "someone might hear you. Oh! What's that?" For with a shrill scream a great bird had risen from the branches of a tree just ahead and flown squawking into the air.

"That's supper!" chuckled the old soldier, and raising his gun he took aim and fired. There was a sharp crash as the bullet struck home, then down fell a large reddish fowl.

"Well?" the fowl rasped sulkily, as Prince Tatters and Grampa ran forward, "what am I supposed to do now? I've never been shot before."

"A bird that's shot is not supposed to do anything," said the old soldier severely.

"Oh," sighed the bird, "that's easy!" and putting down its head, it lay quietly on its side.

"It's a rooster!" exclaimed the Prince, touching it with one hand, "an iron rooster!" At this the bird sprang up indignantly.

"You may shoot me if you want, but I'll not lie here and let you call me names," it shrilled angrily. "Where are your eyes? Can't you see I'm a weather cock?"

"Do you suppose I'd have wasted a good bullet on you if I had? I may have an iron constitution but I don't eat cast iron birds," sniffed Grampa. "What do you mean, flying through this forest deceiving hungry travellers?"

"I don't know what I mean," replied the weather cock calmly, "for I've only been alive since last night. What do you mean yourself, pray? Must everyone have a meaning like a riddle?"

Grampa stroked his whiskers thoughtfully over this remark.

"But how did you come to be alive?" asked the Prince, leaning on his red umbrella and regarding the bird with deep interest—for even in Oz weather cocks usually stick to their poles.

"There was a storm," explained the cock, lifting one claw, "lightning, thunder, wind and rain. One minute I was whirling around on the top of my barn and next minute I was spinning through space. Then all at once I came in contact with a live wire, there was a flash, I was charged with a strange force and to my infinite amazement I found that my wings would work and that I could crow. So I crew and flew and flew and crew, till I fell exhausted in this forest."

"Humph!" grunted Grampa. "A likely story. In the first place there are no live wires in Oz and—"

"Oz!" screeched the weather cock, "I didn't say Oz. I was on a barn near Chicago when the storm broke. Have you never heard of Chicago, you odd looking, old creature?"

"Never," answered Grampa emphatically, "but wherever you started from, you're in Oz now and you might as well get used to it. Come along, Tatters. There's nothing to be gained by arguing, it only makes me hungry."

"But tell me," the weather cock fluttered into the air, "what am I to do with my life?"

"Keep it—if you can," chuckled the old soldier and started off between the trees. But Tatters was loath to leave this singular bird.

"Let him come with us Grampa," coaxed the Prince. "He won't need anything to eat and he might help us find the fortune."

"Yes, do," crowed the weather cock. "I can waken you in the morning, tell you which way the wind blows and fall upon the heads of your enemies. Have you any enemies?" the weather cock asked hopefully.

"Not yet," murmured the Prince, looking ahead into the shadows,—"but—"

"Shouldn't wonder if he would make a good fighter," reflected Grampa, half closing his eyes. "Never saw a cock yet that wasn't game. Do you agree to join this company, obey all commands and go by the name of Bill?"

"I'll go by the name of Bill, but what name shall I come by," asked the weather cock, putting its head on one side.

"The same, you iron idiot!" shouted Grampa, who was a bit short tempered. "Do you agree?"

"Yes," crowed the weather cock, putting up his claw solemnly.

"Then forward fly," commanded the old soldier. And up into the air with a rusty creak flung the weather cock and just beneath marched Grampa and the Prince. As they progressed through the ever darkening forest, Tatters told Bill of the great storm in Ragbad, how he was seeking his father's head and his own fortune.

"Your father lost his head in the same storm I found my life," wheezed the weather cock earnestly, "so it is only fair that I should help you."

"Hah! We shall be helped by fair means or fowl!" chuckled the old soldier, who would have his little joke—but it was lost on Bill, who was already looking around for the King's head and the fortune. And though he was not quite sure what a fortune was, he felt confident that he should find one. It had grown so dark by now that Grampa soon called a halt. Under a tall blue tree the little company made camp. Bill was most helpful in collecting wood and Prince Tatters put up the red umbrella, which was so large that it served them admirably for a tent. A little beyond the rim of the umbrella Grampa kindled a fire, and after a cozy supper of toasted sandwiches the old soldier unbuckled his leg and he and Prince Tatters settled down to a quiet game of scrum. Bill flew to the top of the blue tree to observe the wind and the weather, and nothing could have been more peaceful. The stars twinkled merrily above, the fire crackled cheerily below and Tatters had just beaten Grampa two games to one, when a hundred little snaps in the underbrush made them turn in alarm.

"Great gum drops!" gasped the old soldier, jumping to his foot.

Tatters snatched up the umbrella and, using it for a shield, began to back away, for in the circle of the firelight and completely surrounding the blue tree stood a company of bandits. They were tall and terrible, with great slouch hats and blue boots. Pistols and daggers by the dozen bristled in their belts and nothing could have been fiercer than their whiskered faces and scowling brows.

For a moment no one spoke. Grampa frowned angrily and Prince Tatters tried to look as if he was not scared. As usual, Bill was calm.

"Are you going to stop here and let them call you gum drops?" sneered the leader, plucking a dagger from his boot. He took one stride forward, then pitched on his face and lay perfectly still—for the weather cock, convinced that this was an enemy, had fallen hard upon his head. The suddenness of the blow surprised the outlaws and while they drew back in confusion Grampa leaned down, seized his wooden leg and buckling it on as he ran, joined Prince Tatters, who by this time had his back against the tree.

"Go it Bill!" shouted the old soldier, laying about with his drum sticks.

"Here I go by the name of Bill!" screeched the excited weather cock, rising into the air again. "Here I come by the name of Bill. Sucumb, you blue monster!" And down went a second bandit. This enraged the others, and though Prince Tatters poked away valiantly with the big umbrella, and Grampa knocked out three of the outlaws with his drum sticks and Bill fell upon the heads of two more, they were hopelessly outnumbered. In a minute more they were overpowered, bound with heavy ropes and dragged through the forest to the bandits' camp. Even the weather cock swung head down from the belt of one of the robbers.

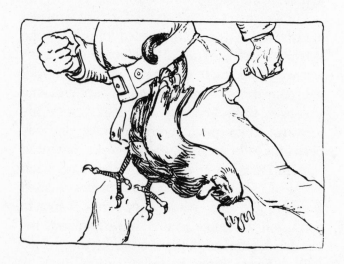

CHAPTER 4
The Baffled Bandits

"I'M SO disappointed I could cry," blub-
bered the robber chief, pulling out his
red handkerchief. "Shake them again Skally,
shake them hard!" Before him on the ground
lay the few possessions of Grampa and Tatters—
an old silver watch, the four-pence, a rusty
pen knife and two copper medals. The chief
had recovered from the terrible blow of the cast
iron weather cock, but had a large black lump
over one eye. Bill, who insisted on crowing in
a dozen different keys, had been muffled in the
bandit's cloak and put under a rock.

"I told you they were a poor lot," sniffed
Skally, but nevertheless, he seized first Grampa

33

and then Tatters and shook them violently by the heels. This he could easily do, being eight feet tall and exceedingly muscular. Two red gum drops rolled out of Grampa's pocket, but that was all.

"And they're not even frightened," complained the bandit in a grieved voice, as Skally set the two roughly on their feet.

"Frightened!" puffed Grampa indignantly. (After the two terrible shakings he had only breath enough to puff.) "You didn't think a flock of bush-whacking bandits like you could frighten an old soldier like me, and a young Prince like Tatters, did you?"

"Prince!" gasped the bandit, blinking at Tatters through the smoke of the wood fire, while the rest of the outlaws began to slap their knees and roar with merriment.

"Yes, Prince," shrilled Grampa, "and don't make faces at me, you ugly villain."

"Well!" roared the chief, after another long look at Tatters, "he may be a Prince to his mother, but he's a pain in the eye to me!"

"Then shut your eyes," advised Grampa promptly. "I'd do it for you if I were not tied up. In a fair fight I'd beat you any day."

"We've taken everything they have. Shall we hang them or let them go?" asked Skally in a bored voice.

"No you haven't," screamed Grampa defiantly. "No you haven't. Take my picture you scoundrel! Take my rheumatism! Take my advice and clear out of this forest before I report you to the Princess of Oz."

Even Prince Tatters, who really was frightened at the fierce appearance of the bandit, had to laugh a little at the surprised expression on the chief's face as the old soldier continued to stamp and scold. And the more Grampa scolded the more cheerful the bandit became.

"He reminds me of my old father," he remarked in an admiring undertone to Skally.

"Does your old father know you're a bandit?" shouted Grampa sternly, "holding up honest adventurers and getting your living by breaking the law?"

"Father always told me to take things easy," replied the chief, popping one of Grampa's gum drops into his mouth. " 'Vaga,' he said to me over and over again, 'always take things easy, my boy,' and I do," grinned the robber wickedly. "But business is mighty slow in this forest lately. Kings and Princes are getting poorer and poorer every day. Look at him!" He waved scornfully at Tatters. "Not worth a shoe button and the whole week it has been the same story. All we got to-day was a wizard, but he was as false as his whiskers—couldn't even change leaves to gold or sticks to precious stones. All he had with him was a bottle of patent medicine. Now medicine," yawned Vaga, touching with his boot a long green bottle that lay with a heap of rubbish near the fire, "is something I never take."

"But I thought wizards were not allowed to practice magic in Oz," put in Tatters, surprised into speech by the bandit's last statement. "It's against the law isn't it?"

"So are bandits!" roared Vaga. "But I'm here just the same, my boy, taking things easy, and when I've saved up enough I'm going to open an Inn and take things easier still."

"Another way to rob honest travellers," groaned the old soldier, "but now, as you've taken our four-pence and our time, untie these bonds and we'll return to our camp."

"Let him tell his story," suggested Skally, "it might entertain us and they certainly owe us something for all this trouble."

"No, I've decided to make outlaws of them," announced Vaga calmly. "The old one is a fine fighter and can be a father to me; the young one would frighten anybody; as for the cast iron bird it can be melted up into bullets."

"What shall we do now?" whispered Tatters, seizing Grampa's arm. The old soldier winked encouragingly.

"Not bad at all," he murmured aloud, as if he were half pleased at the idea of being a bandit. "Plenty of fighting and it's as good a way as any to make a fortune. Swear us in Mr. Vagabandit, swear us in my son!"

The bandit chief was surprised and overjoyed at Grampa's change of heart. He immediately ordered Skally to untie the captives. Each was given a black mask and a dagger and, having raised their hands and solemnly agreed to break every law in Oz, they were welcomed with cheers and shouts into the outlaw band. After the excitement had died down, they all gathered about the fire and Grampa told them the history of Ragbad, how he had got his game leg and of the nine hundred and eighty great battles he had fought in. The bandits listened attentively at first, but the old soldier's recital was so long that presently one and then another of the bandits fell asleep, and by the time Grampa had reached the nine hundredth battle the whole company lay sprawled about the fire, snoring like good fellows instead of bad ones. Prince Tatters, his head on the skin of the old thread bear, was asleep too.

"More ways than one of winning a battle," chuckled the old soldier, smiling behind his whiskers. First, he recovered his watch, medals and the four-pence. They were still on the ground beside Vaga. Protruding from the robber's pocket was a rough blue pouch. Very carefully the old soldier drew it out. "This will pay for the shakings," said Grampa, stowing it away in his game leg. "I'll sample the soundrel's tobacco when we're well out of this." As he straightened up the long, green bottle of patent medicine caught his eye. "I'll take this along too," he muttered, sticking it in his pocket. "Maybe it will help my rheumatism."

The fire had died down and it was so dark and forbidding in the blue forest that Grampa decided to snatch a few hours' rest before making an escape. Stretching unconcernedly beside long-legged Skally he fell into a deep and peaceful slumber. And so well trained was this old campaigner that in two hours, exactly, he awoke. The sun had not yet risen, but in the dim gray light of early morning Grampa could make out the forms of the sleeping bandits. Stepping softly, so as not to waken them, he touched Tatters on the shoulder. The Prince started up in alarm, but when Grampa, with fingers to his lipis, motioned for him to come he seized his red umbrella and tiptoed after him.

"Have I lived to this age to be an old father to a bandit?" puffed Grampa indignantly as they hurried along. He shook his fist over his shoulder. "Farther and farther away is what I'll be." Grampa laughed a little at his joke. "But we can't go without Bill," he muttered suddenly, as they passed the rock under which the robbers had thrust the valiant weather cock. With some difficulty they lifted off the rock and, first whispering strict orders for silence, unwound Bill from the various coats and cloaks. Then Tatters, fearing the creak of Bill's wings would arouse the bandits, stuck him under one arm.

"Wish I knew where they kept their supplies," whispered the old soldier as they pushed on through the heavy underbrush and made their way around gnarled old trees. "My teeth need some exercise."

"What a dreadful lot of crows there are in this forest," mused the Prince, who had scarcely heard Grampa's last remark. "Why the trees are black with them!"

"Well, do you expect me to eat crow?" sniffed the old soldier, waving his sword to disperse a flock of the birds that were circling around his head.

"No, but—" Tatters got no further, for at that instant crows of an entirely different nature made them both leap into the air. The sun had risen and as the first rays penetrated into the dim forest Bill flew out of Tatters' arms and, perching on a low branch, burst into such a brazen clamor of cock-a-doodle-doos that the whole forest rang with it.

"Hush! Halt! Stop that alarm!" gasped Grampa. "Now, you've done it!"

"Oh, Bill, how could you!" groaned the Prince. Snatching off the skin of the thread bear, he flung it over the iron weather cock and seizing him unceremoniously began to run after Grampa. They had already put a goodly distance between themselves and the bandits, but a few minutes after Bill's crowing shots came echoing through the wood and the next instant they could hear the outlaws crashing through the brush. They sounded like a herd of elephants.

"We'll have to hide," panted the old soldier. "Here, crawl into this hollow tree." Without a moment's hesitation, Grampa dove into the tree himself and Tatters, taking a firmer hold on Bill and the red umbrella, followed.

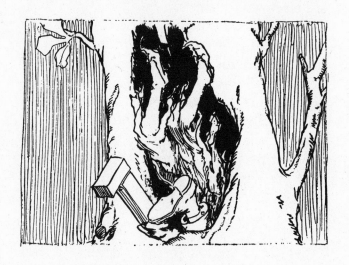

"Is there room?" gasped the Prince. "Grampa, are you there?" But Grampa was not there. Neither, for that matter, was Tatters himself, for his feet instead of resting on earth, rested on nothing. A great wind whistled past his ears and blew his hair straight on end.

"The temperature's falling!" The voice of the weather cock came stuffily through the bear skin.

"Everything's falling!" gasped the Prince of Ragbad, hugging Bill and the red umbrella close to his chest. "Everything!"

40

The Baffled Bandits

You can easily understand what had happened. There was *no bottom* to the hollow tree. When Grampa, Prince Tatters and Bill crawled into the hole, they simply disappeared. They dropped—down—down—down!

CHAPTER 5

Down the Hollow Tree

NOW falling, when you first start, is a hair-raising business, but after you have fallen for a mile and twenty minutes and nothing serious happens you grow rather used to the feel of it. And that's how it was with Tatters.

"Bill," he shouted presently—he had to shout for the rush of air carried away his words as fast as they were spoken—"Bill, where do you suppose we're falling to?"

42

"South by West," crowed the weather cock promptly. The Prince would have liked to continue the conversation, but it took too much breath, so he began planning how he should land without breaking Grampa, for certainly Grampa was somewhere below. Rather sorrowfully he reflected that they were falling farther away from the Emerald City every minute. He wondered where his father's head was, and what Mrs Sew-and-Sew would think if she could see them tumbling down this hollow tree. Would it never grow lighter? Would they never reach the bottom and what would happen when they did? Just as he came to this point in his wonderings, Tatters dropped into a clump of pink bushes so hard that for several seconds he could do nothing but gasp.

"Well," crowed Bill, beginning to flutter restlessly about in the bear-skin, "are we here?"

"Yes, thanks to you. You're discharged!" roared the old soldier, as Prince Tatters picked up himself and his red umbrella. Grampa had been less fortunate in his landing. He sat in the middle of a cinder path, blinking rapidly, and as Bill scrambled out of the bear-skin and hopped after Tatters, he raised his gun threateningly.

"You're discharged without pay," repeated Grampa angrily. "What do you mean by crowing and betraying us to the enemy?"

"I couldn't help it," answered Bill in an

43

injured tone. "It is the nature of a cock to crow and I've helped the sun to rise."

"And us to fall," scolded Grampa. "Well, you're discharged!" Rolling over with a groan, he drew the bottle of patent medicine from his pocket. Fortunately it was not broken, but it had made a dreadful dent in Grampa.

"But wherever in Oz are we?" exclaimed Prince Tatters, trying to change the subject, for he did not intend to have Bill sent off in this hasty fashion. The old soldier pretended not to hear and continued to stare resentfully at the bottle of medicine. On one side was pasted a green label and Tatters looking over his shoulder read, with some surprise:

Sure cure for everything.
Follow the directions on the bottle.

Beneath in tiny printing was a long list of ailments. Grampa ran his finger hastily down the list until he came to breaks, sprains and bruises. "One spoonfull immediately after fall-ing," directed the bottle. Without a word, Grampa took a tin spoon from his knapsack, uncorked the bottle and swallowed the dose.

"Why, it's the wizard's medicine!" cried Tatters, watching him anxiously, for no sooner was the stuff down than a broad grin overspread Grampa's face. "Good thing I brought it along— works just like magic—never know I'd fallen," puffed Grampa, completely restored to good

humor. "Better have some, boys." The old soldier smiled at his companions.

Tatters, who was not hurt at all, shook his head and Bill, who had flown into the air to examine the bottle, shook his wings.

"Well—good-bye!" wheezed the weather cock hoarsely. "You don't need me to direct you now—you can follow the directions on the bottle. Here I go," he finished sulkily, "here I go by the name of Bill!"

"Don't go," begged Tatters, looking pleadingly at the old soldier. Now Grampa, remembering the splendid way Bill had fallen upon the bandits, had already relented, but he never apologized.

"Company fall in!" he commanded gruffly, putting the wizard's medicine in his pocket. Tatters winked at Bill and Bill, muttering something about having fallen in already, began to march down the cinder path. They had dropped into a small park surrounded by a hedge that grew up as high as they could see. A soft glow shone through the hedge and by its rosy light the three adventurers began to examine their surroundings with great interest. The park itself was pretty enough, but after marching entirely around it and finding no break in the hedge, Grampa looked rather worried.

"It's a good enough place for a picnic," puffed the old soldier, dusting his game leg, "but then we're not on a picnic!"

"No," sighed Tatters, sinking down on a bench, "we're not on a picnic, for there's nothing to eat."

"If you were made of iron like I am you would never be hungry," crowed the weather cock, proudly. "I am glad I am cast in iron, but what shall we do now, Mr Grampa?"

"Fly up and see how high the hedge is," directed the old soldier, "while Tatters and I try to cut an opening." Pleased to be of some service, Bill hurled himself upward, and Grampa with his sword and Tatters with his rusty pen knife began hacking at the hedge. But as fast as they cut away the twigs, others grew and after ten minutes hard work they gave up in despair. Then down came Bill with the discouraging news that he had flown as high as he could, and the top of the hedge was

still nowhere in sight. "But the wind is blowing north," finished the weather cock calmly.

"Bother the wind!" sputtered Grampa.

"Must we stay here till we starve," groaned Tatters, "and never find my father's head or the fortune at all?"

"Fortune," repeated Bill, putting his head on one side as if the word brought something to his mind. "Don't worry about that, for I have already found the fortune." And while Grampa and the Prince stared at him in amazement, he touched with his claw a tiny golden key. It was suspended on a thin chain round his neck and neither of them had noticed it before.

"Why, where did you get that?" asked Tatters.

"I picked it out of the robber chief's pocket,"

explained Bill, rolling his eyes from one to the other.

"You'd make a fine bandit," chuckled Grampa, "but that's not a fortune, old fellow!"

"Then what *is* a fortune?" asked Bill, looking terribly disappointed.

Grampa pulled his whiskers thoughtfully, for a fortune, when you come right down to it, is hard to explain.

"Well," he began slowly, "it might be gold, or jewels, or land. Anything precious and rare," he finished hastily.

"Isn't this gold?" demanded Bill, holding up the key.

"Oh, Grandpa, maybe it's the key to the bandit's treasure chest," interrupted Tatters excitedly. "Let's go back and hunt for it."

"And how are you going?" inquired the old soldier sarcastically. "Falling down trees is easy enough, but you can't fall up trees like you can fall up steps. However," he added quickly, seeing Tatters' downcast face, "there must be some way out. Let's look again."

"I'm going to keep this key," mused Tatters in a more cheerful voice, "for I believe it will help us." He gave Bill a little pat on the head as he took the chain off his neck, and somewhat comforted, but still mightily puzzled, the iron weather cock hopped after Grampa. This time they circled the hedge more slowly, the old soldier taking one side and Tatters and Bill the other. It was Bill who made the discovery—for shining through the leaves on the left side the weather cock caught the gleam of gold!

"The fortune!" he crowed loudly. "The fortune!"

It was not a fortune, but a golden gate, and pushing aside the leaves and twigs Grampa and Tatters stared through the bars into the loveliest garden they had ever seen. The gate was unlocked, and when Grampa pressed upon it with his shoulder it swung noiselessly inward. Fairly holding his breath, Tatters stepped in after the old soldier, and Bill had just time to hop thorugh before the gate swung shut again. Grampa gave a low whistle and Tatters an involuntary cry of admiration. Flowering vines and bushes filled the air with a delicate fragrance; paths of silvery sand wound in and out among the trees and arbors; crystal fountains splashed between the flower beds; and bordering each path and grass grown lane were trees glowing with magic lanterns, lanterns that bloomed as gayly as the blossoms themselves and lighted up the garden with a hundred rainbow sheens. It was all so strange and beautiful that Tatters and Grampa scarcely dared breath but Bill, having been alive only two days, seemed to think magic gardens quite usual affairs.

"Come on," he called excitedly, "let's find the fortune!" But a golden sign on the nearest magic tree had caught Tatters' eye and, paying no attention to Bill, he tiptoed over to it.

"This is the Garden of Gorba," announced the sign. "Mystery and magic in all its branches."

Grampa had come up behind Tatters. "Gorba," muttered the old soldier softly. "Now where?" He pulled the bottle of patent medicine from his pocket and squinted first at the sign and then at the bottle. "The same!" puffed Grampa, for written in gold letters at the end of the list of ailments was the name Gorba.

"This must be the garden of the wizard that rascally bandit was telling us about," muttered Grampa uneasily. "He must have been on his way here when they held him up. Maybe he's here now! Hush! Be careful! Watch out now! I wouldn't trust a wizard as far as I could swing a chimney by the smoke!"

CHAPTER 6

The Wizard's Garden

"MAYBE he will tell me where to find my father's head," whispered Tatters excitedly.

"Well," admitted Grampa, starting cautiously down one of the silver paths, "that would be a good turn, but a wizard's more likely to turn us to good gate posts or caterpillars."

"I refuse to be a caterpillar," rasped the weather cock. He had flown down and was hopping close to Grampa's heels. "I'll give him a peck in the eye!" Rattling his iron wings, Bill looked around anxiously.

"Well, don't forget you're under orders," snapped Grampa severely. "No forward falling, crowing or pecking till I give the word, understand?"

"I don't believe he's a bad wizard," observed the Prince quietly, "his garden is too pretty."

"Pretty is as pretty does," sniffed Grampa. "He's practising magic, which is against the law, and you can't get around that, besides—" Just here Grampa trod upon a small flagstone path that led across a broad stretch of lawn and never finished his sentence at all, for the stone rose a foot into the air and started bouncing across the green at such a rate the old soldier teetered backward and forward and did a regular toe dance to keep his balance.

"Wait!" shouted Tatters in alarm, and running after Grampa, himself stepped upon one of the lively flag stones. Up rose the stone and the next thing the Prince of Ragbad was bouncing after the old soldier, waving his red umbrella and calling frantically for Bill. But Bill was already aboard the third stone, and before any of them had sense enough to jump, the stones bounced straight under a silver fountain, dumped off their three startled passengers and went skipping back to their places in the walk.

"Variable winds and heavy showers," crowed Bill dismally.

"Scaps and scribbage!" sputtered the old soldier. "I told you that wizard was a villain.

Company fall out!" he commanded gruffly. This the company lost no time in doing.

"Oh, well," laughed Tatters, rolling from under the drenching spray, "it saves us the trouble of washing our faces. But what made them do it Grampa?"

Grampa gave himself an angry shake and marched stiffly over to the flagstone path. Carved neatly on the last stone were these words:

> Gorba's Stepping Stones,
> Guaranteed for seven centuries.

Stand on the right foot to go East, on the left to go West.

Stand on both feet to go South. To go North stand on your head.

"Well, North's the way we want to go!" cried

Tatters eagerly as Grampa finished reading. "Maybe they'll carry us all the way to Emerald City."

"Not me!" snorted the old soldier, taking a pinch of snuff. "Stand on your head if you like, but I'm going to travel right side up or not at all. Do you want to break your neck?" he demanded indignantly.

"It would be a little rough," admitted Tatters, remembering the way the stones had bumped, "but it's pretty good magic just the same." Grampa grunted contemptuously and tightened the fastenings of his game leg, but even the old soldier could not stay cross long in this enchanting garden, and when a moment later they happened upon a cluster of peach trees he grew quite cheerful again.

"Always did like peaches for breakfast," he sighed, impaling one on his sword. Twirling the sword and taking little bites all round, he looked with half closed eyes down the long vistas of lantern lanes. "I wish Mrs Sew-and-Sew could see this," sighed the old soldier pensively. Tatters nodded, but he was impatient to see more of the wizard's garden, so filling his pocket with peaches, he ran down the narrowest of the lanes after Bill, who had already flown ahead to have another look for the fortune. Opening out from this lane was a smaller and enclosed garden filled with the strangest bushes Tatters ever had seen. Each one grew in the shape of an animal. There were bears, tigers, lions, elephants and deer and the eyes, noses and mouths were marked by blossoms of the proper size and shape, that grew cunningly just where they were needed. They looked so life-like that for a moment the Prince was frightened, but after he had prodded a lion bush with his umbrella and it neither roared nor lashed its green tail he proceeded from one to the other quite as if he were in a museum. And certainly Gorba's animals were queer enough to grace any museum.

"Wonder how he makes 'em grow this way?" murmured Tatters, finishing his last peach.

"Might as well wonder how he happens to be a wizard," chuckled Grampa, who had come up quietly behind him. "Why, this is better than a zoo, it's a whole blooming menagerie, and if we knew the secret of it we could travel all over Oz growing deer and rabbit bushes in the castle gardens and your fortune would be made in no time. But as we don't know the secret of it," concluded Grampa, squinting at his old silver watch, "we'd better forward march and see if we can find a way out of here." With many backward glances, Tatters followed him down another of the lantern lanes, but they had scarcely gone half way when the hoarse voice of the weather cock came screeching overhead.

"The Princess! The Princess! I have found the Princess!" crowed Bill, falling with an iron clang in the path before them.

"Be quiet," warned the old soldier anxiously, "do you want the wizard to get you? Now then, what's all this nonsense about a Princess?" Grampa winked at Tatters and Tatters winked back, for neither of them had much faith in Bill's discoveries. But the weather cock was too excited to mind. Hopping stiffly ahead and pausing every few seconds to urge them forward with a wave of his wing, he led them to the very center of the enchanted garden. There, on a bed of softest moss, surrounded by a rose blown hedge, lay the loveliest little maiden you could ever imagine!

"The Princess," repeated Bill huskily. "The Princess!"

"You're wrong," breathed the old soldier, pushing back his cap and tip-toeing forward, "you're wrong. It's the Queen of the May!" And it surely seemed that Grampa had guessed correctly, for Bill's Princess was a little Lady of Flowers. Her face, hands and neck were of the tiniest white blossoms, her eyes, deep blue violets, her mouth a rose bud and her nose and brows delicately marked with pink stems. Her hair, blowing backward and forward in the fragrant breeze, was the finest spray of flowering fern, and her dress was most enchanting of all. The waist was of every soft, silken flower you could think of, buttoned all the way down the front with pansies, while her skirts—a thick cluster of blossoming vines—fluttered gayly about her tiny lady slippers.

"Why!" exclaimed the Prince of Ragbad, "she's growing in the flower bed. Oh, Grampa, if she were only alive!"

"I wish she were myself," sighed the old soldier. "This wizard must know a deal of magic to grow a little fairy like that. Mind what you're about there," he called sharply to Bill. The weather cock had flown over the hedge and was hopping so close to the flower girl it made Grampa nervous.

"But look!" crowed Bill, "Looky look!" Under the hedge and padlocked to a small iron ring in the ground was a gold watering can. It did not

take Grampa and Tatters long to leap over the hedge after that, for as the old soldier said himself, the wizard was doubtless away and it was their plain duty to see that this little flower

maid had a freshening spray before they left
the garden. First Tatters tried to wrench the
can loose. The golden chain on the padlock was
so slender it should have broken on the first
tug, but it held like iron. Then Grampa tried
his hand, but with no better luck; next both
Grampa and Tatters tugged together, Bill doing
his bit by jerking out the Prince's coat tails.

"More magic!" panted Grampa, sucking his
thumb. "The only way to get it loose is to find
the key."

"The key," shrilled Tatters, suddenly diving
into his pocket. "Why, I wonder if this is the
key?" Jubilantly he produced the tiny gold key
Bill had taken from the bandit and the next
instant he had fitted it in the padlock.

"Vaga must have stolen that from the wizard
when he took the medicine," mused Grampa,
"and that wizard's mighty particular with his
old gold can." He sniffed scornfully as Tatters
slid it from its chain. "Here, I'll fill it at the
fountain."

"But it's already full," answered the Prince
of Ragbad, giving it a little shake.

Running over to the mossy bed, he tilted the
gold can forward and sprayed the little flower
lady from top to toe. Stars! No sooner had the
last drop fallen than a perfectly amazing thing
happened—so amazing that Grampa and Tatters
clutched each other to keep from tumbling over
backwards and Bill flew screaming into the
nearest tree. For the little flower maiden slowly

and gracefully rose from her bed, poised a
moment on tip-toe and then, with a merry little
laugh, bounded over to Grampa and Tatters
and seized their hands. Next thing they were
whirling round and round in the jolliest fashion
imaginable, faster and faster and faster, till
everything grew blurred and all three tumbled
down in a heap.

"Oh, forget-me-nots—isn't that fun!" trilled
the little flower girl, jumping lightly to her
feet. "Oh, I've wanted to do that always!"

"Who—who are you?" gasped Tatters, for
Grampa, between loss of breath and astonishment, was perfectly speechless.

"Why, just my own self," smiled the little
creature, flinging back her feathery hair.

"How do you blow? How do you blow?"
shrieked Bill, falling in a heap beside her.

"He means how do you do," puffed Grampa,
laughing in spite of himself. "You'll have to
excuse him for he's a weather cock and used
to talking to Augusta." Then as the little
maiden still seemed puzzled, Grampa finished
his sentence. "Augusta Wind," chuckled the
old soldier, with a wink that made them all
laugh, except Bill, who continued to regard the
flower girl intently.

"Are you a Princess?" asked Bill, with his
head anxiously on one side.

"No," mused the little girl slowly, "I don't
think I'm a Princess, let—me—see. Oh, I
remember now the old wizard telling the birds

my name was Urtha, because I'm made of earth!"

"Go along with you then," snapped Bill crossly. "We're looking for a Princess."

"Don't mind him," begged Tatters jumping up hastily.

"Tell us about yourself, Miss Posy," cried Grampa, straightening his cap and feeling his game leg slyly. In the dance it had turned completely around. "I declare you're the loveliest little lady I've met in all my travels."

The roses in Urtha's cheeks seemed to grow pinker at Grampa's words.

"There isn't much to tell," she began softly. "I don't seem to remember anything but this garden. I guess I just grew," she finished with a little bounce that sent her skirts flying out in every direction.

"And whatever was in that gold watering can brought you to life. I believe you're a fairy," said the old soldier solemnly.

"No! No!" laughed the little flower girl, seizing a long trailing vine. "I'm just Urtha." And using the vine as a skipping rope she flashed up and down the silver paths so swiftly that it made Tatters and Grampa blink just to follow her dancing steps.

"What are you going to do now that you are alive?" asked Tatters as she paused for a moment beside him.

"Just going to be happy in this garden,"

replied Urtha with a little shake of her lovely fern hair.

"I wish we could stay too," sighed Tatters, for he could think of no end of games he could teach Urtha, and even the Emerald City, he reflected, could not be lovelier than this enchanted garden. Grampa gave a start at Tatters' words and, suddenly recalled to his duty, gathered up his gun and knapsack.

"It's been a pleasure to know you, my dear," said Grampa gallantly, taking off his cap, "but we'll have to be marching on now, for we've a long journey before us."

"Oh!" Urtha gave a little cry of dismay. "Didn't you grow in the garden too?" Grampa shook his head and as quickly as he could told her how King Fumbo had lost his head and how he and Tatters had set out to seek it and the Prince's fortune. Urtha was almost as much puzzled over a fortune as Bill. Indeed, the whole of Grampa's story was confusing—for you see it was the first story the little flower maiden had ever heard. But Prince Tatters and the old soldier interested her tremendously. She touched Grampa's medals shyly and could not admire Tatters' patched and many colored suit enough. As for Bill, she blew him so many kisses that the embarrassed weather cock flew and hid himself in an oleander bush. Saying good-bye to dear little Urtha was a difficult business, but at last Grampa, with a very determined expression, shouldered his gun and Tatters reluctantly picked up his red umbrella.

"Come on!" shouted Bill, impatiently sticking his head out of the bush. "Come on, or we'll never find the head, the fortune and the Princess." As Urtha had not turned out a Princess he had lost all interest in her.

"But I'll miss you," sighed Urtha, and drooped so sadly against a tree that Tatters promptly fell out of line and began to comfort her.

"You won't miss us," said Grampa, looking uneasily at his watch, "you can't miss people you've just met, you know." The old soldier was faced with a problem the like of which he had never before encountered, and he was plainly at a loss to know what to do.

"I've known you longer than anyone else. I've known you my whole life," sighed Urtha wistfully.

"But you've only been alive five minutes," smiled the old soldier indulgently.

"Why don't you join the army like I did?" inquired Bill, who was anxious to be off.

"Oh, couldn't she?" begged Tatters eagerly. Grampa shifted his feet and looked uncertainly at the little flower maiden. She seemed too frail and delicate to set out on a journey of adventure. "But," reflected the old soldier, "if she's a fairy nothing can harm her and if she's not, someone ought to look out for her. As we brought her to life we're responsible."

"Come along with you," cried Grampa recklessly. So away through the wizard's garden marched this strange little army, the patched flag of Ragbad fluttering from the top of Tatters' red umbrella and the little flower maiden falling out of line every few minutes to dance gaily round a tree or skip merrily through a fountain.

She fairly seemed to float above the flowers that blossomed along the way, as her dainty feet slipped from daisy to daisy. Prince Tatters could hardly keep his eyes away from Urtha as she danced along the way. And Grampa smiled happily at the delight of the two happy young people.

CHAPTER 7

The Winding Stairway

IT was twilight in the wizard's garden. All the lanterns burned low and the birds twittered drowsily in the tree tops. Grampa and Tatters sat wearily upon a golden bench—for after a whole day's march they were no nearer the Emerald City than before. Indeed, there seemed no way out of the enchanted garden. They had lunched satisfactorily on the fruit of a bread and butter bush, and Grampa's knapsack was full of nicely spread slices, but for all that each one of them felt tired and downhearted.

Urtha, on the contrary, was as fresh and merry as in the morning and, seated under a willow tree, was weaving a daisy chain for Bill.

"She is certainly a fairy," mused Grampa and absently pulling a blossom from a near-by bush he popped it into his mouth. "We'll take her back to Ragbad, my boy, and won't she liven up the old castle! I tell you, now—" Suddenly Grampa stopped speaking and clapped his hand to his belt. His eyes grew rounder and rounder and Tatters, turning to see why he did not finish his sentence, gave a little scream of fright.

"Help!" called the Prince of Ragbad in an agonized voice. "Help! Help!" Urtha was beside him in an instant, while Bill circled wildly overhead.

"He's growing," breathed the little flower maid softly.

"Yes," groaned Tatters distractedly, "he's growing a chimney!" And Tatters was quite right. Not only was the old soldier growing a chimney, but a bay window as well. The chimney had knocked off his cap and grown brick by brick as the horrified Prince looked on. The bay window, of fancy wood-work and glass, jutted out at least three feet beyond Grampa's waist line. (The old soldier had always been proud of his slim figure.)

"Give me my pipe," panted Grampa in a choked voice. He had no idea what was happening, but felt too terribly dreadful for words. Tatters sank on one knee, snatched the pipe from its place in his game leg and lit it with trembling fingers. Then it was that he caught sight of the sign on the bush beside Grampa. "House plants," said the sign distinctly.

"Oh!" wailed the Prince, suddenly remembering that Grampa had eaten one of the blossoms, "you've eaten a house plant and there's a chimney sticking out of your head."

"There *is*!" roared Grampa, puffing away at his pipe in great agitation. "Well, that's what comes of this pesky magic. A chim-nee! Well, I'll try to bear it like a soldier," he finished grimly. A perfect cloud of smoke rose from the chimney at these valiant words. Too overcome for speech, Tatters covered his face.

"Don't you care!" cried Urtha, flinging her arms 'round Grampa's neck. "It's a sweet little chimney, and *so* becoming!"

"The wind is blowing North," crowed Bill, disconsolately following the direction of the smoke as it curled up Grampa's chimney. "If I see this wizard I'll fall on his head. I'll give him a peck in the eye, five pecks, but say!" Bill paused in his circling and swooped down upon the old soldier. "How about the medicine?" Grampa and Tatters had forgotten all about the wizard's green bottle, but at Bill's words the old soldier drew it quickly from his pocket.

"I don't believe there's any cure for chimneys," puffed Grampa, running his finger anxiously down the list. He was so nervous that his hands shook. To tell the truth he expected to grow a flight of steps or a veranda any minute.

"Here, let me look," begged Tatters, snatching the bottle from Grampa. But though there was everything on the green label from ear ache to lumbago, no mention was made of chimneys or bay windows at all.

"But it says 'cure for everything,' " insisted Bill, perching stubbornly on Grampa's shoulder.

"This is worse than a battle!" moaned Grampa, rolling up his eyes. "I'm poisoned, that's what I am."

"Poisoned!" cried Bill triumphantly. "Then find the cure for poison." Hurriedly Tatters consulted the label. "For poison of any nature, two drops on the head," directed the bottle. So

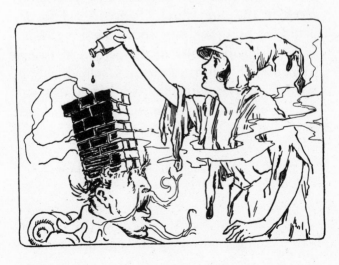

while Urtha and Bill watched nervously, Tatters uncorked the bottle and let two drops of the magic liquid fall down Grampa's chimney. There was a slight sizzle. Tatters rubbed his eyes and Bill gave a crow of delight. The chimney had melted and the bay window was gone and the gallant old soldier quite himself again. Urtha was so happy that she danced all the way round the golden bench and Grampa jumped up and ran to look at himself in a little pond.

"No worse for it," mused the old soldier, stroking the top of his head tenderly and patting his belt with great satisfaction, "but that's the last bite I'll take in this garden." As Grampa turned to go, a particularly bright little flower bed caught his attention. The flowers grew right before his eyes, dropped off their stems and were immediately succeeded by other ones. Even in the dim lantern light the old soldier could see that they were spelling out messages.

"Gorba will return to the garden at twelve o'clock." This announcement bloomed gaily in red tulips, and while the old soldier was still staring at it in astonishment, the tulips faded away and another sentence formed in the bed:

Who stays all night shall leave here never,
  He'll be a lantern tree forever!

In yellow daffodils, the sentence danced before Grampa's eyes. "A life sentence!" panted the old soldier wildly, and without waiting for more he plunged across the garden.

"Tatters! Bill! Urtha!" shouted Grampa, his own voice hoarse with excitement. "The wizard's coming back and we've got to get out of this garden or be lantern trees forever!"

"Forever!" gasped the Prince of Ragbad, who had scarcely recovered from the chimney business. As fast as he could, Grampa told of the flower messages, and when they hurried back to the bed, a pansy sentence had already grown there.

"Good-night," said the pansies politely, then fluttering off their stems, blew like gay little butterflies across the lawn.

"*Good* night!" choked Grampa bitterly. "It's the worst night I ever heard of. I won't be rooted to the spot, nor a tree for any old wizard wizzing. Come on! Company 'tenshun!"

"Here I come by the name of Bill," crowed the weather cock, hurling into the air.

"But what are we coming to?" panted Tatters, shouldering his red umbrella dutifully, while Urtha kept anxiously beside him.

"We're going back to those stepping stones," puffed Grampa, stumping along determinedly. The lanterns winked lower and lower and soon it was so dark and shadowy they lost the path entirely. Smothering his alarm, Grampa marched doggedly on, bumping into benches and trees, but never once pausing.

"They ought to be here some place," wheezed

the old soldier and then stopped with a grunt, for he had run plump into an iron railing in the dark.

"What is it?" whispered Tatters, straining his eyes in the gathering gloom.

"Why, it's a flight of steps," cried Grampa in the next breath. Feeling for the gate, he entered the little enclosure and struck a match. By the flickering light, he saw six circular golden steps and on the top one in jewelled letters were just three words: "Gorba's Winding Stairway." Then the match sputtered and went out.

"Winding stairway," puffed the old soldier joyfully. "Why, this must be the way out. They wind up, I'll bet a gum drop! Get aboard everybody. Hurry! Here Loveliness!" Taking Urtha's hand, Grampa guided her up the first step. Tatters stood on the second with Bill on his shoulder. Grampa mounted quickly to the top and striking another match looked anxiously for directions. There were no more inscriptions, but under Gorba's name was a tiny gold handle. The match was burning lower and lower and just as it went out Grampa seized the handle and turned it sharply to the left. Then—"Great Gollywockers!" gasped the old soldier, clutching at the rail. "It's winding down!"

Poor Grampa, in his hurry, had turned the handle the wrong way, and next instant the brave little company were whirling down the wizard's winding stairway, 'round and 'round, down and down, 'round and down, down and 'round, until they were too dizzy to know where they were going.

"Hold on!" called Grampa wildly. "Hold on! Hold on! Hold on!" And hold on was about all they could do.

CHAPTER 8

Strange Happenings in Perhaps City

O N THE same bright morning that Grampa
and Tatters started from Ragbad, the
Peer of Perhaps City sat cozily breakfasting
with Percy Vere. Percy was a poet and attended
to all the guess work in Perhaps City. True he
was a terribly forgetful poet, but he did the
best he could and was a prime favorite with
the old mountain monarch. Perhaps City itself
is a tall, towered city of gold set high in the
Maybe Mountains of Oz. So steep and craggy
are its peaks that none of the dwellers in the

city ever descended into the valleys below. Indeed there is little need of it, for life in Perhaps City, owing to the jolly nature and good management of old Peer Haps, is so delightfully entertaining that the people have no desire to leave. The Happsies themselves are of the light-hearted and old-fashioned race of Winkies, who in olden Oz times, settled all the countries of the East. The only one who ever left the city at all was Abrog, the High Sky prophet of the realm, and to his goings and comings no one paid much attention, for he was a queer, silent old man, who spoke but once a year and only then to prophesy as to the weather, crops and important events that would take place in the town.

So far these events had all been happy and fortunate ones, and on this sunshiny morning, old Peer Haps, buttering his muffins in his cozy breakfast room, felt so well pleased and content with his lot that he fairly beamed upon Percy Vere.

For his part, Percy Vere always was happy and, beaming back at the king, he shook his long locks out of his eye and laughed merrily at old Peer. Percy Vere always felt that his patron enjoyed his breakfast particularly if Percy opened the proceedings with a verse, so he sang, as breakfast was served, this ditty:

"Oh, muffins mellow light and clear,
Fit diet for a mountaineer;

73

Oh, muffins pale and yellow!
Oh, muffins sweet to sniff and eat,
How you refresh a—a—"

The poet's merry blue eyes grew round and puzzled, as they always did when he forgot a word.

"Fellow!" chuckled the Peer, taking a sip of coffee. "Percy, my child, you are ridiculish!"

"I am ridiculish, I know it;
A young, a poor forgetful—er"

"Poet!" spluttered Peer Haps, with another chuckle.

"Thanks old Nutmeg!" sighed Percy, helping himself to another muffin. "You always know what I mean."

"*Nut* Meg!" roared Peer Haps. He never got over being amused at Percy's informal way of addressing him. "*Nut* Meg! Well, I'll be grated!" And immediately he was, for at that very moment, the folding doors flew open and in rushed Abrog the prophet.

"Greater than all other Rulers in Oz, great of the greatest!" began the old man, salaaming before Peer Haps, "a great misfortune threatens, approaches, is about to take place."

"What?" cried the Peer, choking on the last bit of his muffin. It was strange enough to have Abrog speak at all when it was not the day for prophecy, but to have him speak in this foreboding fashion was simply too terrible.

"Speak out! Speak up!" cried the Forgetful Poet, leaping to his feet:

"Speak out, speak up
And then get hence,
We cannot stand this dire—
    this dire, this dire—"

"Suspense," finished Peer Haps automatically. "Yes, speak up, fellow!" he cried anxiously.

"In four days, a monster will marry the Princess!" wailed Abrog, pulling his peaked cap down over his eyes. "In four days, four days, four days!" And having said this, he began to gallop 'round the breakfast table, Peer Haps and the Forgetful Poet right after him. You, yourself, can imagine the effect of such a message on the merry old Peer of Perhaps City. Why, he prized the little Princess above all his possessions, yes, even above his yellow hen who was a brick layer and laid gold bricks instead of eggs. Indeed, she had done more than anyone else to lay the foundation of his fortune.

"What kind of a m-monster?" stuttered the Forgetful Poet, waving his muffin.

"Where is my daughter now?" demanded Peer Haps, seizing Abrog by the whiskers, for there seemed no other way of stopping him. Abrog waved feebly toward the window and, rushing across the room, the Peer and the poet stared out into the garden where the sweetest little Princess in all the countries of the East was gathering roses. She waved gaily to the two in the window, and, with a shudder, Peer Haps turned back to Abrog.

"Let me see the prophecy," he demanded, holding out his hand. Abrog produced a crumpled parchment and after one glance the old Peer covered his face and sank groaning into his enormous arm chair. The Forgetful Poet had read over his shoulder and instantly burst into all the melancholy poems he knew. "Oh, hush!" begged the old monarch at last, "and you," he waved wildly at the prophet, "can you do nothing but run 'round that table like a merry-go-round goat?"

"I could marry the Princess myself," rasped Abrog, coming to a sudden standstill before the Peer. "If she were already married to me, a monster could not marry her," he leered triumphantly.

"To *you!*" shrieked Percy Vere, crushing his muffin to a pulp.

"You weazened, wild, old, whiskered dunce,
Be off! Be gone! Get out, at—at—at—
   at—"

Percy began hopping about on one foot groaning, "What's the word, what's the word?"

"Once!" finished Peer Haps, mopping his forehead and glaring at Abrog, for he was stunned at the old man's suggestion. "It wouldn't do at all," he muttered gloomily.

"Why, you're a thousand years old if you're a day, and she's the only daughter I've got."

"Well, you won't have her long," sneered Abrog, gathering his robe about him. His black eyes gleamed wickedly from beneath their bushy brows. He was furiously angry, but quickly hiding his feelings he began to move slowly toward the door. Halfway there he paused. "Since you refuse my first solution of the difficulty, I will endeavor to think of another one. I used to know a little magic," he wheezed craftily. "I will retire to my tower to think."

Peer Haps nodded absently. He was too dazed to think himself and could only mutter over and over, "A monster! A monster! My daughter! A monster!"

"The fellow's a fool!" choked Percy Vere. "He's as full of ideas as a dish pan. Why he's a monster himself!"

"But there's something in what he says," groaned the old Peer unhappily. "If my daughter were already married when this monster came, he could not carry her off. I have it! Percy, we'll marry the Princess at once, to the likeliest lad in Perhaps City."

"To me!" cried the Forgetful Poet, tossing back his long locks and sticking out his chest complacently.

"Well—er," the old monarch looked a trifle embarrassed, "you're hardly the man to marry and settle down to a humdrum royal existence. I was thinking of young Perix."

"You're right," agreed Percy, mollified at once. "Marriage would interfere with my career, O Peer. Shall I fetch our pretty little Princess?"

"Yes, call her at once," begged Peer Haps, clasping and unclasping his hands, "but don't frighten her, Percy my boy, no talk of marriage or monsters!"

Percy felt that the only thing he could do, under the circumstances, was to lapse into verse.

> "I go, I go, on heel and toe
> To fetch the sweetest girl I know,
> The Princess of Perhaps City,
> As sweet as sugar full of tea!"

caroled the Forgetful Poet, bounding through the door into the garden. Peer Haps smiled

faintly, then remembering the monster, frowned and began drumming nervously on the arm of his chair. He did not even look up when the yellow hen hopped into the room, and, with a self-conscious cluck, laid a gold brick on the mantel.

"What's the matter?" asked the hen sulkily.

"Everything!" groaned Peer Haps, straining his eyes for the first sign of Percy and the Princess. "Everything!" At that instant Percy rushed back.

"The Princess is lost, gone, mislaid!" cried the Forgetful Poet, crossing his eyes in his extreme agitation.

"You speak as if she were an egg," clucked the yellow hen, but no one paid any attention to her and in a huff the spoiled creature flew out the window and dropped a gold brick on the head of the chief gardener. But no one, except the chief gardener, paid any attention to this either, for Peer Haps had raised such a clamor over the disappearance of his daughter that the whole castle was in an uproar. Indeed in five minutes more every woman, man and child in Perhaps City had joined in the search for the missing Princess. After they had searched high and low, and everywhere else for that matter, Percy suddenly bethought himself of the prophet and, rushing up the fifty steps to his tower, thumped hard upon the door. There was no answer. Percy flung the door open and there was no prophet. Abrog was gone too!

In the face of this new calamity the dreadful prophecy about the monster was almost forgotten. Peer Haps sank down upon his throne and in spite of his sixty years and three hundred pounds wept like a baby.

"He's perfectly perfidious!" exclaimed Percy Vere, who was entirely out of breath from the steps. All the courtiers solemnly shook their heads

> "A villain old and hideous,
> And perfectly perfidious,
> Has run off with our daughter.
> What shall be done to him, O Peer,
> This prophesighing profiteer
> Deserves both death and—and—"

"Slaughter," sobbed Peer Haps convulsively. Then mopping his face he sat up. "Someone must follow him at once and bring her back!" thundered the old monarch. "A thousand gold bricks to the man who brings her back. A thousand gold bricks and the Princess' hand in marriage!" At this there was a great shuffling of feet and the young men of Perhaps City began to exchange uneasy glances.

"Down the mountain?" asked Perix faintly.

"Where else?" demanded Peer Haps, glaring angrily at the young nobleman whom he had intended for his daughter.

"But we might be dashed to pieces. It is terribly unsafe," stuttered Perix unhappily. All the other Happsies began to shake their heads and murmur sadly, "Unsafe, very unsafe!"

"Well, how about my daughter?" roared the poor monarch, puffing out his cheeks. "Will no one go after my daughter?" There was more

shuffling of feet, but not a voice was raised. We must not be too hard on these young Happsies, remembering that in all their lives and in the lives of their fathers and grandfathers no one had ever descended Maybe Mountain excepting Abrog the old prophet.

"I'll go myself!" spluttered Peer Haps explosively. But as he arose with a great groan, the Forgetful Poet rushed forward and embraced as much of the Peer as his arms would circle.

"You'd be broken to bits!" cried Percy distractedly. "Suppose you stumbled. I, I will go and find the Princess and this meddling, miserable prophet."

"You! Why you'll forget what you're after before you start," sneered Perix disagreeably.

"As to that," said Percy, snapping his fingers under the young fellow's nose, "I may forget a word now and then, but I don't forget how to act when my King is in trouble!"

"Hurrah!" shouted the gardener, throwing up his hat. He had recovered from the shock of the gold brick. "Hurrah for Percy Vere; he's the bravest of the lot!"

"But how will you go?" quavered Peer Haps. He was torn between relief at Percy's brave offer and sorrow at the thought of losing his prime and favorite companion.

"Here's how," cried the valiant Poet. Rushing down the golden steps of the palace, Percy leaped over the gate and plunged recklessly down the steep mountain side. Percy was well accustomed to hill-climbing and met with no mishap as he plunged downward.

CHAPTER 9

Dorothy Meets a New Celebrity

DOROTHY had been to see the Tin Woodman and now, with Toto, her small shaggy dog, running at her side, was skipping merrily down one of the wide Winkie Lanes.

"I think Nick Chopper looks very well, don't you Toto?" said Dorothy, tickling his ear with a long feathery weed.

"Woof!" barked Toto reproachfully. Toto— like all other dogs in Oz—could talk if he wanted to, but Toto, being originally from

Kansas, preferred his own language. Just then, seeing a lively baconfly, Toto gave another bark and dashed across a daisy field. Away fluttered the baconfly, and you have no idea how fast these little rascals can flutter, and away, his ears flapping with excitement, pounded Toto, and away after Toto ran Dorothy, for she was always in fear of losing her reckless little pet. Up and down, here and there, 'round and 'round, darted the mischievous baconfly, until Toto's tongue hung out and he simply panted with exhaustion. Then with a spiteful sputter, the baconfly disappeared under a rhinestone, and after scratching and whining and even growling a little, Toto gave up the chase and trotted rather sheepishly back to Dorothy.

"That was really too bad of you Toto," panted the little girl reprovingly. "You wouldn't eat a poor little baconfly, would you?"

"Woof, gr-rr woof!" sulked Toto, which was Kansas for "You *bet* I would!" Pretending not to understand this last remark, Dorothy fanned herself with her broad straw hat and started slowly back toward the lane. But the baconfly had led them such a round-about chase that when she did come to the lane she turned in exactly the opposite direction from the way she had intended, and instead of walking toward the Emerald City she began walking away from it. But as neither she nor Toto was aware of this fact, they progressed most cheerfully, Dorothy carrying on a one-sided conversation with the saucy little bow-wow. Occasionally Toto would bark or wag his tail, but most of the time he listened in superior silence to the little girl's chatter of the fun they had had in Nick Chopper's tin castle.

Now how Nick Chopper came to have a castle is a story in itself, for Nick has, in the course of his strange and interesting life, risen from a wood-chopper to Emperor of all the Winkies and from an ordinary blood and bone man to a real celebrity of tin. Yes, Nick is entirely a man of tin, as you can see by referring to any of the histories of Oz. In these same histories it is recorded how a wicked witch enchanted Nick's ax, so that first it cut off his legs, then his arms and finally his body and head. But you cannot kill a good Ozman like Nick Chopper and after each accident he hied him to a tin-smith for repairs. First the tin-smith made him tin legs, then tin arms, next a tin body and at last a tin head, so that he was completely a man of tin. And this same little Dorothy, on her first trip to Oz, had discovered the Tin Woodman, rusting in a forest, had oiled up his joints and taken him to the Emerald City itself. There the Wizard of Oz had given him a warm, red plush heart, which he still has and since then Nick has been in almost every important adventure that has happened in the wonderful Land of Oz. Ozma, the little fairy ruler of Oz, finding Nick so dependable and so unusual, has made him Emperor of the

East, and the loyal little Winkies have built him a splendid tin castle in the center of their pleasant yellow country.

Dorothy herself was first blown to Oz in a Kansas cyclone and after a great many visits to this delightful country, determined to stay for good. So Ozma, with the help of her magic belt, transported Dorothy and Uncle Henry and Aunt Em and Toto to the Land of Oz. Uncle Henry and Aunt Em have a comfortable little farm just outside of the Emerald City, but Dorothy and Toto have a cunning apartment in the Emerald Palace itself, for Ozma cannot bear to have Dorothy far away. The two girls— for Ozma herself is only a little girl fairy—have been through so many adventures together that they are almost inseparable, and to show her love and affection for this little girl from the United States Ozma has made Dorothy a Royal Princess of Oz.

But through all her honors and adventures Dorothy has remained the same jolly little girl she was in Kansas. Every now and then she puts aside her silk court frocks, slips into an old gingham dress and steals off for a visit to some of her friends in the country.

"We'll soon be at the Scarecrow's, Toto; shall you like that?" she asked, after skipping along for five whole minutes without speaking. "Perhaps he'll have corn muffins and honey and—Whatever's that?"

"Little girl! Little girl!" A voice came echoing

high and clear down the sunlit lane. Toto pricked up his ears, and Dorothy, shading her eyes, turned in the direction of the voice. Running toward her was a young man clothed all in buff—an extremely excited and agitated young man—and by the time he reached Dorothy and Toto he was perfectly breathless.

"Well—" began Dorothy, hardly knowing what else to say.

"Not very well, thank you," puffed the young man, slapping at his face with a yellow silk handkerchief. On closer inspection Dorothy saw that his handsome suit was torn and muddied and the young man himself exceedingly scratched and weary.

"I am most unhappy," he continued, regarding her mournfully. "At least, when I can remember to be. It is hard to be unhappy in a lovely country like this."

"Then why do you try to remember to be?" asked Dorothy with a little laugh, while Toto made a playful dash at the stranger's heels.

"A great deal depends on my remembering," explained the young man eagerly. "If I forget to be unhappy I may forget why I fell down the mountain and why I am wandering in this strange country without friends or food."

"Well, why are you?" Dorothy could control her curiosity no longer.

"I am seeking a Princess," replied the youth solemnly.

"A Princess! Well, will I do?" Dorothy smiled

mischievously and while the stranger stared at her, round-eyed, she made him her prettiest court bow. The result was extremely funny. The Forgetful Poet—for of course you have guessed all along that it was he—extended his arms toward Toto and cried accusingly:

> "I looked the maiden in the eye,
> I looked her up and down,
> She says she is a Princess,
> But, she hasn't any—any—?"

Toto barked indignantly at this limping poetry.

"I suppose you mean crown," giggled Dorothy. "Yes I have too, but it's at home, in Ozma's castle."

> "The crown is in the castle,
> The castle's in the town;
> The town is in the land of Oz,
> But how about her—her—"

He stared helplessly at Dorothy's gingham dress and, with another little scream of laughter, Dorothy finished his verse. "Gown!" spluttered the little girl. "Do you always talk like that?"

"Pretty often," admitted Percy Vere apologetically. "You see, I am a poet. And I know who you are now. You're Princess Dorothy herself!" He smiled so charmingly as he said this that Dorothy could not help smiling back.

"I've read all about you in Peer Haps' history books," confided Percy triumphantly. "Shall I address you as Princess?" As he asked this question the troubled expression returned to his eyes. "You haven't seen a Princess anywhere around here have you?" he added anxiously. Dorothy shook her head and Toto began sniffing under all the bushes as if he expected to find a Princess in any one of them.

> "A little Princess,
>   Passing fair,
> With rosy cheeks
>   And yellow—yellow—"

"Hair," put in Dorothy quickly. "Who is she? Who are you and how did she get lost? Let's sit down and then you can tell me all about it."

"He's exactly like a puzzle," thought Dorothy,

with an amused little sniff. So Percy Vere sat down beside her under a spreading jelly tree and as quickly as he could he told of the strange happenings in Perhaps City, of the prophecy about the monster, of the strange conduct of old Abrog, the Prophet, and finally of the disappearance of both the Princess and the Prophet.

Percy himself had fallen down the steep craggy sides of Maybe Mountain, arriving in a scratched and bruised heap at the bottom. All morning he had been wandering through the fields and lanes of the Winkie land and Dorothy was the first person he had encountered.

"Well, I think you were just splendid," breathed the little girl, as the Forgetful Poet finished his story. Percy had tried to gloss over the young men's refusal to go in search of the Princess, but Dorothy had guessed quite correctly what had happened.

"I'll bet that old prophet carried her off himself," she declared positively.

"I think so two,
I think so three,
I think so four,
Where can they—?"

Percy mopped his brow and looked appealingly at the little girl.

"Be," supplied Dorothy obligingly. "I'm sure I don't know, but we can soon find out. You

91

just come to the Emerald City with me and
we'll look in Ozma's magic picture."

"Why you are wise
    As you are pretty;
Let's hasten to
    The Emerald City!"

Smiling all over because he had actually
finished his own verse, the Forgetful Poet
helped Dorothy to her feet and both started
gaily down the lane, Dorothy telling the poet
all about the interesting folk in the capitol and
Percy Vere telling Dorothy all about the City
of Gold on Maybe Mountain. Dorothy's idea of
looking in Ozma's picture, like all of her other
ideas, was a mighty good one, for this picture
has a magical power enabling a person to see
whomever he wishes, so that one look would
disclose the whereabouts of the lost Princess of
Perhaps City. But at every step, they were
putting a longer distance between themselves
and that look. For at every step, thanks to that
little baconfly, they were going farther and
farther away from the Emerald City of Oz.

They had eaten the lunch the Tin Woodman
had thoughtfully put up for Dorothy, and now,
as the afternoon shadows began to lengthen,
the little girl looked anxiously ahead for familiar
landmarks. But instead the lane—which should
have led straight to the Scarecrow's tower,
which is halfway between the Tin Woodman's

Palace and the Emerald City—the lane suddenly came to a stop in a scraggly little woods.

"That's funny!" mused Dorothy, looking around in surprise.

"Are we lost?" asked Percy, leaning wearily against a tree.

> "Hello! Hello, why here's a sign
> Tacked up upon this prickly—prickly—"

Without bothering to finish the verse, Dorothy hurried over to the pine.

"Look out for the Runaway," advised the sign, in large red letters.

"Runaway!" cried Dorothy, snatching Toto up in her arms. "Good gracious! I wonder what kind of a runaway it is?" They were not long left in doubt, for while Percy was still staring nervously all 'round, there came a hiss and a snap and 'round a big rock shot the runaway itself, scooping up the two travellers before they had time to even wink a single eyelash.

"This is p-perfectly preposterous," blustered the Forgetful Poet. Both he and Dorothy were sitting in the middle of the runaway and Percy Vere hastily slipped his arm around the little girl to keep her from falling off. The runaway road itself was humping along like some dreadful sort of serpent, jouncing and bouncing them so terribly that talking was almost impossible.

"Wonder where it's running!" gasped Dorothy, hugging Toto so tight he began to growl a little. From somewhere ahead a gritty voice answered her.

"I'm running straight to a pepper mine," roared the runaway, "and you'll make a handsome pair of pepper diggers."

"P-pepper diggers!" groaned Percy Vere.

"Pepper diggers, not that please,
The very idea makes me, makes me—"

"Ha-ha-ka kachoo," sneezed Percy miserably.

"Pepper doesn't grow in mines. It's a plant," shouted Dorothy indignantly.

"Well, this pepper mine of mine was planted," replied the road, twisting 'round to stare at Dorothy with its stony eyes. Neither Dorothy nor the Forgetful Poet answered this time, for the bumping and bouncing had grown so much worse that it was all they could do to

hold on to each other and keep from biting their tongues off. Nothing like this had ever happened to the Forgetful Poet before. He was simply stunned. But Dorothy had been in so many strange adventures and had had so many odd experiences in the land of Oz, that she was already planning to outwit the runaway.

"It wouldn't be safe to jump off," thought the little girl, "for we'd probably be broken to bits, but—" Her eyes travelled upward to the trees and bushes that were flashing past as the runaway flung itself recklessly through the forest—"If we caught hold of a low branch the old road would go on without us," she reflected triumphantly.

As well as she could, for bumps and bounces, she whispered her plan to Percy Vere. He nodded enthusiastically and transferred Toto to his blouse, so that Dorothy would have both hands free. Then, when a huge tree loomed up ahead, they both began to count, and as its branches stretched over the runaway, they hurled themselves upward and held on for dear life. Beneath slithered the road and not until the last yellow length of it had flashed by did Dorothy and Percy Vere let go. Percy dropped to the ground first, gently lifted Dorothy down, and took the frightened, wiggling little Toto out of his blouse.

"Whew!" breathed Dorothy, leaning dizzily against Percy, "that's the worst ride I've had for a long time. Wonder where we are?"

"Do—we—do—this—often?" panted the Forgetful Poet, looking at Dorothy with round eyes. "I'm perfectly pulverized!"

"Well, I never met a runaway before," confessed Dorothy, "but you never can tell what's going to happen in Oz, so first thing we'd better do is to find out where we are!"

"We're in a forest dark and deep,
I hope the bears are all—are all—"

"Asleep! So do I!" sighed Dorothy, and began tip-toeing along under the great lonesome trees, Toto keeping close at her side and Percy Vere treading softly behind her.

CHAPTER 10

Prince Forge John
of Fire Island

B EFORE Grampa and his little company
had recovered from the shock of winding
down instead of up, the strange stairway
gathered itself together, and, with a sudden
jerk, shook them all off.

"Break ranks!" roared the old soldier, kicking
out wildly with his game leg.

"I don't want to break my ranks," said Bill
crossly. Tatters and Urtha were too startled to
say anything and for a few seconds they simply
fell in surprised silence. The hollow down

which they were tumbling was wide and dimly lighted with a soft, spooky glow. The air was thick and heavy and they were falling much slower than Grampa and Tatters had fallen down the hollow tree. First fell Urtha, her flowery skirts fluttering gracefully around her; then fell Tatters, clinging to Bill with one arm and his red umbrella with the other; then the old soldier, his gun, drum, sword and knapsack rattling like a box full of marbles.

"I feel exactly like a butterfly. Are we flying, dear Mr Soldier?" laughed the flower maiden presently.

"No, my poor child," puffed Grampa, staring down at her anxiously. "We're falling!"

"Falling asleep?" asked Urtha contentedly.

"Depends on how we land," groaned the old soldier, and suddenly remembering his last landing he snatched the wizard's medicine bottle from his pocket.

"Is there anything on the label about falling?" panted Tatters, who was close enough to notice the old soldier's action. Grampa held the bottle close to his eyes, and though reading while falling is one of the hardest things I know of to do, after a deal of squinting the old soldier read out the following: "For falling hairs, one drop in full glass of water!"

"But we're not hares," wheezed Bill indignantly.

"And if our hair stopped falling and we fell

on, we'd be scalped!" puffed Grampa hoarsely. "Besides there isn't any water, so there's nothing to do but fall!"

"Stormy weather! Stormy weather!" predicted Bill gloomily. "Look out below, look out, look out, look out!" As the weather cock came to his last look out, the air grew suddenly lighter, the speed of the four fallers increased and next thing, with a great splash and splutter, they had plunged into a deep underground lake. Blowing like a porpoise, Grampa rose to the surface.

"One drop in water," choked the old soldier and, treading water furiously, he began to look around for his little army. In the dim green light he could see Urtha floating like a tiny island of flowers on the top of the water—her fine spray of hair spread out 'round her lovely little face. A short distance away Tatters was making frantic efforts to keep afloat but, with the iron weather cock and the enormous umbrella, it was a difficult business and every few minutes the poor Prince of Ragbad would disappear under the waves. Grampa himself, handicapped as he was by a game leg and so many weapons, found swimming a dreadful exertion and by the time he reached Tatters he was completely exhausted. He still grasped the wizard's bottle in one hand.

"Wet—very wet!" The head of Bill appeared above the water and then went under, as Tatters took another drive toward the bottom.

"Grampa, I'm drowning!" gulped the poor Prince, reappearing for a second on the surface. It never occurred to the Prince to drop Bill or his father's umbrella. Grampa himself had shipped so much water he had no breath to speak, but he flung his hand out desperately toward the Prince and, as luck would have it, it was the hand holding the wizard's medicine.

"D—don't drown!" begged Grampa, his eye fixed desperately on the green label. "Wait, there's a cure for it." Treading water again, he clutched Tatters by the hair and pressed the bottle to his lips. "One swallow and you'll swim like a fish," promised Grampa.

"My head's swimming already," muttered Tatters weakly. It was all the Prince could do to get the stuff down, for he had swallowed quarts of the lake already. Grampa was so interested in watching the effects of the dose that he forgot to move his feet and went down himself. But just as the water closed over his head he put the wizard's bottle to his own lips, took a hasty mouthful and jammed in the cork. Immediately he bobbed to the surface and, with a great sigh of relief, saw Tatters floating on top of the waves, Bill perched precariously upon his chest. Grampa felt as buoyant as a cork and, using his gun as an oar, steered toward Tatters and Urtha and soon all three were bobbing along side by side.

"This medicine's the only good thing that wizard ever invented," said Grampa, sticking the bottle through his belt. "Feeling better, old boy?"

Tatters shook his head feebly. He could not help thinking how far out of their way they had fallen, and how very far they were from the Emerald City and even from Ragbad itself. He blinked hastily at the thought of Mrs Sew-and-Sew and the cozy red castle on the hill, and he hoped Pudge had remembered to feed his pigeons. Tatters himself never expected to see them again. Only Urtha seemed really to be enjoying the adventure. Her little flower face was wreathed in smiles and her lovely flower frock fairly sparkled with freshness.

"Isn't this fun!" she kept repeating merrily. "Isn't this fun?" Grampa nodded, but not very enthusiastically.

"Do you think we'll ever get back on top again?" asked Tatters gloomily.

"Of course," spluttered Grampa. "We've fallen down about as far as we can fall and from now on things will take an upward turn, you see. Hello, this water's kinda hot! Great swordfish, what's that noise?"

"The fortune! The fortune!" shrieked Bill, jumping up and down upon Tatters' thin chest and ducking the Prince at every jump. "The fortune!"

With a great effort, Grampa sat up in the water, which was already beginning to steam, and then fell backward with a terrific splash.

"Halt!" commanded Grampa, trying to push against the current with his sword. "Stop! Halt!" A great roaring was in their ears and the green light had changed to a red hot glow. Now Tatters sat up. Then he, too, began to kick wildly about in an effort to stop himself. And no wonder! They were being carried straight toward a roaring red island of fire!

"The fortune! The fortune!" screeched Bill, more excited than ever.

"Fortune!" groaned Grampa, reaching out to catch Urtha, who was floating rapidly past. "Misfortune! Halt! Stop! Everybody back!"

"Better stop backing and look on that bottle," gulped the Prince of Ragbad. "Better see if there's any cure for—for this!" He waved desperately ahead. And Grampa, with a little choke of fright, pulled out the wizard's medicine. "Burns, scalds and heat strokes," faltered Grampa. "Well, we'd better take the cure for all three." A teaspoonful was prescribed in each case and with trembling hands the old soldier measured out the doses. Bill could not swallow, so the old soldier dashed the medicine over his head.

"I think you're a fairy," puffed Grampa, throwing a dose in the face of the surprised little flower girl, "but if anything should happen I'd never forgive myself." Tatters came next and by this time the water was so hot that Grampa himself began to groan with discomfort. So he hastily swallowed his three spoonfuls, corked the bottle and prepared for the worst. But immediately everything grew better. The waves of heat from the island seemed only pleasant breezes now and the steaming water did not even feel hot. Before they had time to wonder at all this, they were washed up on the burning sands of Fire Island itself.

"Is it the fortune?" asked Bill, hopping out of Tatters' arms. "You said land—or gold, and this is a golden land."

Grampa was too dazed to answer. Finding himself completely fire proof was strange enough, but actually walking on an island of fire seemed unbelievable.

"Wonder what Pudge would say to this," mused Grampa, as Tatters rushed over to his side. Urtha was already dancing about on the glowing sands as happily as she had danced in the wizard's garden.

"Here come the firemen!" cried Prince

Tatters, and rather anxiously the old soldier turned to meet the islanders. The People of Fire Island were as interesting and unusual as their island, being entirely of red and blue flames, and so light upon their feet they fairly flashed about over the glowing rocks.

"Shall I fall on their heads?" inquired Bill. "Is it a fight?"

"No," answered Grampa, squinting a bit from the glare, "I believe they're friendly." And the old soldier was right, for as the Fire Islanders came nearer they waved their arms gaily and seemed delighted with the unusual appearance of their visitors. A little ahead of the others strode a tall man, who was made entirely of glowing, red hot iron. Except for this face, he might have been any village blacksmith and his face was so round and jolly that Tatters immediately took heart.

"Prince Forge John the First!" called two small flame pages, as the Fire Monarch reached the party on the beach. Prince Forge John bowed, Grampa saluted, Bill crowed and Ur- tha—breaking off a flowery spray from her skirts—held it out prettily to the ruler of Fire Island.

"What a charming little fairy!" cried Prince Forge John in his hot crackling voice. "And you," he turned pleased eyes upon Grampa and Tatters, "how brave you look, and *it*," with a wave at the weather cock, "how beautiful it is—all of splendid iron!"

"Thanks," crowed Bill. "I'm useful, too. If you will tell me where to find the head, the Princess and the fortune, I'll tell you which way the wind blows. Head? Fortune? Princess?" finished Bill, as if he were repeating a lesson

Prince Forge John looked so confused at this speech that Grampa stepped forward and hastily explained all that had happened since King Fumbo had lost his head, ending up with the wizard's garden, the discovery of Urtha and their fortunate use of Gorba's medicine.

"H-m!" mused Prince Forge John, rubbing his iron chin. "So you're seeking the head of this lad's father and the lad himself seeks a fortune and a Princess? Well, I have not seen the King's head, but the Prince may stay here with us, marry one of our Fire Maidens and make a fortune in the fire works. There's many a fortune been snatched from the fire. How would you like that, my boy?"

"Yes, do stay and marry me," cried one of the little flame maidens, running impulsively up to the Prince. "You are so odd and you look so interesting!"

Tatters looked terribly embarrassed, for he was fearful that the maiden would scorch his nose. "I—I must find my father's head first," stuttered the Prince, backing away uneasily, "and if your Majesty could tell us of a way back to Oz—" Tatters bowed again and looked appealingly at Grampa.

"Well, you might go up in smoke," suggested

Prince Forge John slowly. "I think, myself, that this wizard's medicine will wear off presently and then you'll all burn up."

"Oh," groaned the old soldier, snatching out his handkerchief, "why do you think such terrible thoughts?"

"Would it hurt?" breathed Urtha, who hated to see anyone unhappy.

"Is there no fire escape?" choked Tatters, with bulging eyes.

Prince Forge John shook his head. "I'd like to help you," he murmured gravely, "but you are so strangely made I don't see how I can. Better just stay on here. Burning's not so bad and I think you'd burn a long time." Several of the Fire Islanders nodded as the Prince said this, but Grampa and Tatters could find no consolation in such a prospect.

"And marching North seemed *so* easy!" wailed poor Tatters, leaning heavily on his red umbrella.

"Never mind," sighed the old soldier, "I'll think of something else. Let's jump back in the water," he proposed brightly.

"But if the medicine wears off boiling would be just as bad as burning," objected Tatters, with a little shudder.

"That's so," admitted Grampa. "It seems, my boy, that every cup of soup has at least one fly!"

"There's a fly on your nose," screeched Bill, hopping up and down. And so there was—a saucy little fire fly. There were fire flies everywhere—darting here and there among the fire flowers and over the fields of waving fire weeds.

"Better stay," repeated Prince Forge John hospitably. "Anyway let us show you a bit of the island."

Grampa nodded, for he did not know what else to do, and so he and the others followed sadly after the Prince and his cortege. There were no houses on Fire Island, but each flame family had its own open fire place. Between stretched meadows of clear blue flame and many beautiful gardens, where, from flowing beds of red hot coals, lovely fire flowers arose. The stems were of green flame, the tops of yellow, blue and red. The Prince picked a bouquet of these strange posies for Urtha and, to Grampa's surprise, the fire flowers neither burned the little flower girl nor went out in her hands.

If it had not been for the dreadful thought of burning up that hung over them, the old soldier and Tatters might have enjoyed their trip across the island. But as it was they got little pleasure from it. Even Prince Forge John's fire works, where all the hearth fires and kitchen fires are manufactured and the Fourth of July roman candles and sparklers are made, aroused in them no enthusiasm. When they reached the other side of the island, the Prince offered each member of the party a box of fire

crackers for refreshments and this made
Grampa smile in spite of his worry.

"No use setting ourselves off before our
time!" chuckled the old soldier, handing them
back with a bow. The Prince looked a little
hurt, but he and the rest of his company ate
up their fire crackers with relish and after
Prince Forge John had finished his sixteenth
box he had a sudden idea.

"I've thought of a way to save you," cried
Prince Forge John, fairly crackling with pleasure. "You can just go to Blazes!"

"What?" shouted Grampa, who, being in the
army, thought he was insulted.

"Yes," repeated Forge John calmly. "You
must go to Blazes. See that dark house across
the waters there? Well, you'll find him on the
other side of that."

Grampa shaded his eyes and, looking across the green, sulphurous waters surrounding Fire Island, made out a great tower of Darkness. It was quite easy to see, for every other place was lighted with the ruddy glow from the island.

"Fetch the boat," ordered the Prince briskly, and while Grampa and Tatters were still gazing in stupefaction at the tower, several of the fire men began shoving an iron boat down the beach. Unceremoniously Forge John took them by the arms and helped them in. To tell the truth, he was growing sleepy and anxious to be rid of these singular visitors.

"The flower fairy may stay," he yawned graciously, but Urtha had no such intention. Gently disengaging herself from a group of the fire maidens, she ran after the boat and sprang lightly in beside Tatters.

"What do you mean? Where are we going? Hold on here!" blustered the old soldier. But Prince Forge John merely waved his firm arms and the two fire men began to row away as fast as they could.

"Good-bye," called the Prince, with another yawn. "I'm sorry you wouldn't stay and burn with us."

"We're going to blazes, to blazes, to blazes!" crowed Bill, who had flown up into the bow of the boat.

"That's right," crackled the flame man nearest to Tatters. "He'll soon send you up."

"But who—who is Blazes?" asked the Prince

111

of Ragbad, stretching out both his hands imploringly.

"The keeper of the volcano," answered the second rower, looking at Tatters intently.

"Lightning, thunder, hot winds and earth-quakes!" crowed the weather cock wildly.

Grampa flopped hopelessly into the bottom of the boat.

CHAPTER 11

Into the Volcano

B Y THE time Grampa had recovered enough
to sit up the boat was scraping on the
black rocks at the foot of the dark tower.

"Cinders! Soot!" called the rowers loudly. In
answer to their hail a door opened cautiously
and the keepers of the dark tower peered out.

"What's wanted?" asked the first hoarsely,
while the second swung his dark lantern toward
the party in the boat.

"Take these men to Blazes and tell him to
send 'em up!" directed the flame men together
and, almost pushing Grampa and his little

company from the boat, they jumped in and started to row back to their island. The dark tower was wet and clammy and made of moss that soaked up the rays of light from Fire Island as a sponge soaks up water. The keepers of the tower themselves looked burnt out and cindery and far from agreeable.

"You go!" said Soot, after a contemptuous glance at the newcomers. "I've got to keep the light out."

"All right!" agreed Cinders. "Come on you, whatever you are!" There was no way to get back to Fire Island, so Grampa motioned for the others to come and in silence they followed Cinders over the black, slippery rocks. Bill perched on Grampa's shoulder and Tatters held fast to Urtha, who for the first time seemed a little frightened.

"Being alive is so strange," sighed the little flower girl, stepping along tremulously.

"It's not always like this," whispered the Prince comfortingly. He was terribly frightened himself, but resolved to be as brave as he could before this lovely little lady of flowers. The dark tower seemed to be on the mainland of this queer underground country and, after a short march over the rocks, they came to a steep gray mountain. There was a door in the center and Cinders hammered on this with a poker he carried under one arm. The door opened immediately and a hot red glare smote the travellers in the face.

"John says to send these creatures up," grumbled Cinders, backing out of the light.

"I hope that medicine's still working!" groaned Grampa. "Do you still feel cool?"

"Pretty cool," faltered the Prince of Ragbad. "But—"

"Come in," roared the huge fireman, who had opened the door, "do you want to give me chill?" Snatching Tatters by one hand and Urtha by the other, he jerked them through the door and Grampa, seeing that Cinders was about to slam it shut, sprang in quickly after them. Blazes was about twice as tall as the men on Fire Island and his flaming face was cruel and ugly.

"So you're to be sent up?" he sneered, staring curiously at the bewildered little company. "Well, you're not worth an eruption, but orders are orders, so up you go!"

Grampa could find no words to answer, for his eyes were glued in horror upon the boiling lake of lava, churning about a few feet below. Thick green smoke curled up toward them in clouds and just as he was about to order a hasty retreat to the door the keeper of the volcano seized a forty-foot poker and plunged it into the lake.

Next instant it had risen to the top, caught the four fire-proof travellers in its sulphurous waves and hurled itself frothing and bubbling to the top of the earth. Being erupted from a volcano is such a noisy, smothering, altogether

terrifying experience that Grampa and his little army could not have told what was happening had they tried. And had it not been for Gorba's medicine they would have blown clear out of the story, but, thanks to the medicine, the boiling lava did not injure them and having hurled them from the middle of the earth and some fifty feet higher than the earth, the liquid immediately surrounding them began to harden and form a flying island.

Of course Grampa and Tatters were too dizzy to know this and the first indication they had that the eruption was over, was a dreadful bounce and a perfect shower of water. The water brought them to their senses and— fearfully opening their eyes—they looked around. Horrors! The volcano was in the Kingdom of Ev, on the other side of the Deadly

Desert, and had flung them clear into the Nonestic Ocean itself! This great body of water lies far to the Northwest and mighty few Ozites have ever reached its shores.

"Well," coughed Grampa, rubbing his game leg vigorously, "I thought we were goners, but I see we are survivors. Are you all right? Are you all here?"

Urtha shook her lovely fern hair out of her eyes and, strange as it may seem, the little flower girl had come through the eruption without crushing a single posy.

"Fair and cooler!" wheezed Bill, hopping up on a little ridge of the hardened lava.

"But how did we get here?" asked Tatters, rubbing his eyes.

"You'll have to ask Blazes," puffed Grampa, "but I must say I prefer water to fire." Already the spirits of the old soldier were beginning to rise. "We may be far from home, but we're on top again and still moving." Grampa took a few marching steps and waved his sword.

"And what are those?" asked Urtha, standing on tip-toe to point at the stars. In the wizard's garden there had been no sky. Tatters explained as best he could and the little flower girl clasped her hands and gazed up in delight. "They're sky flowers," she confided to Bill, but the weather cock was too busy looking for the fortune to answer.

"Seems to me we're shipwrecked," observed Tatters gloomily. Their little island was bobbing up and down on top of the waves and there was no land of any kind in sight. But Grampa, who had been investigating the contents of his knapsack, gave a little chuckle. The bread and butter they had picked in the wizard's garden—not being entirely fire proof—was nicely toasted and looked so crisp and inviting that it made Grampa's mouth water.

"What you fussing about?" said the old soldier, winking at the Prince. " 'Tisn't everybody can have their supper cooked in a volcano." He handed Tatters a great pile of the toast and after the Prince of Ragbad had eaten a dozen slices, he began to feel more cheerful himself.

"All we need is a little sleep," yawned the old soldier, after they had finished off the toast, for neither Bill nor Urtha needed food. "If Bill will keep watch, you and I had better turn in, for there's no knowing what may happen to-morrow."

"I'll keep watch," promised Bill readily.

"Hush!" warned Grampa suddenly, for Urtha, wearied by her strange adventures, had fallen fast asleep in the middle of counting the stars and lay in a fragrant heap, her lovely violet eyes closed tight and all the big and little posies that made up the wonderful little flower girl herself were asleep too.

"If she hadn't been a fairy," whispered Grampa, looking down at her affectionately, "she would have wilted long ago. We must take good care of her, my boy, for I doubt if there's as lovely a little lady anywhere else in Oz."

"She's the only luck we've had," mused Tatters, "and I wish—" The Prince looked up at the stars and did not finish his sentence but, rolling up the skin of the old thread bear, he made a pillow for Urtha's head and he and Grampa went tip-toeing to the other side of the island and stretched themselves on the ground. The motion of the little island, as it rode lightly over the waves, was very soothing and before long the old soldier and the young prince were sound asleep too, leaving only the weather cock on guard. And Bill, in all the years he had spent on the barn near Chicago, had never felt so important. Perched on the highest ridge of the island, he kept a sharp look-out in all directions, scanning the tumbling waters of the Nonestic Ocean for signs of a fortune and a Princess and talking softly to himself in the starlight.

Grampa was having a fine dream. He was being presented at court and was just about to shake hands with Princess Ozma herself, when he was wakened by a ton of kitchen tins falling down a mountainside. Or that's what it sounded like to Grampa. Leaping to his feet, the old soldier snatched up his gun. Tatters and Urtha were both sitting bolt upright, rubbing their eyes.

"It's Bill!" yawned the Prince sleepily. With

an exclamation of disgust, the old soldier threw down his gun and covered his ears. The weather cock was indulging in his morning crow and helping the sun to rise. Just as Grampa thought he could not stand it another minute, the frightful clamor ceased.

"The sun has risen," announced Bill calmly, "and there's land ahead!"

It was a bit foggy but, crowding to the edge of the island, the little company saw that they were being carried straight toward a land of ice and snow. Tatters and Urtha had never seen snow before, for there is no snow in Oz, but Grampa had read all about such things in Fumbo's books and, while he was explaining, the little island bumped on the snowy shores of this strange ice-bound land.

"All off!" cried Grampa, seizing Urtha by the hand. Tatters ran back for his umbrella and the skin of the old thread bear; then jumped after Grampa and the flower maiden.

"Colder and colder!" predicted Bill, flying after the Prince and settling on the branches of an ice-covered tree. But Tatters was not thinking of the weather. With round eyes, he was studying a huge sign that stretched between two tall hemlocks.

"The Illustrious Island of Isa Poso," announced the sign, and in smaller letters, "Beware of the dragon."

"Great Gollywockers!" gasped the old soldier,

reading over Tatters' shoulder. "Can't they give a feller a rest?"

"What's a dragon?" asked Urtha, touching Tatters on the arm.

CHAPTER 12

The Island of Isa Poso

W HILE Tatters was still studying the sign and explaining a dragon to Urtha, the old soldier stepped over to another tree where an even larger sign was displayed. This is what it said:

REWARD!
One-half the kingdom and the hand of the
Princess Poso to the slayer of the dragon
Enorma.
Chin Chilly the Third,
King of Isa Poso.

"Hah," cried Grampa, with a little skip, "this is more like it!"

"Like what?" asked Tatters, blowing on his stiff fingers.

"Like olden times. In my youth," said Grampa solemnly, "young lads served in the armies of strange kings, slew monsters and were rewarded with half the kingdom and the Princess' hand. Let us immediately slay this dragon, my boy, and win the reward. Then all that will be left for us to do will be to find your father's head."

"And I'll find the dragon," volunteered the weather cock, rising into the frosty air.

"What shall I do?" asked Urtha, running up to the old soldier.

"Just be your lovely little self," smiled Grampa, "and stay where we can see you. Why, just to look at you makes me feel like a conquering army with banners flying."

Urtha was so happy at Grampa's neat little speech that she blew him a kiss and began dancing in circles over the shimmery snow and wherever Urtha's foot rested the snow melted and flowers sprang up, until there were circles of posies pricked out against the snow. Grampa and Tatters were so interested that they almost forgot the icy wind that was blowing over this white, frozen land. But soon the Prince, who in spite of the skin of the thread bear was thinly clad, began to shiver and the old soldier to shake in good earnest. First he stood on the other because that was his game leg and not subject to frost bites.

"A game leg's a mighty fortunate thing," wheezed Grampa huskily, "but I wish we were like Urtha—then we wouldn't feel this pesky wind. Let's march on, for if we stay here we'll freeze stiff." Marching on an empty stomach through a strange freezing land was not the pleasantest thing in the world but both Grampa and Tatters stepped out bravely, the young Prince smiling over his shoulder every few minutes at the little flower maiden. "It's a lucky thing we're not being followed," whispered Grampa, and it certainly was—for after them, in a tell-tale row, pansies, tulips, daffodils and forget-me-nots marked out the steps of the light footed little flower fairy.

"I hope we track down this dragon soon," groaned Tatters, pausing to stamp his foot and rub the end of his nose. Icicles were forming on Grampa's whiskers and the sun, flashing on the snow, almost blinded the gallant old soldier. He was almost ready to quit.

"No wonder the king calls himself Chin Chilly," chattered Grampa dismally. "My chin's chilly too; I'm chilly all over. Urtha, my dear, do you see anything that looks like a dragon?"

"I see a bright light," called Urtha, who was dancing ahead of the shivering adventurers.

"I feel a warm wind!" cried the Prince of Ragbad excitedly.

"The dragon! The dragon!" screamed the

weathercock, appearing suddenly over the top of a bleak, icy hill. Before Bill's warning had died away, the dragon itself hove into view and, with a great roar, came tobogganing down upon the frightened little company like a scenic railway train. Urtha jumped behind Tatters, Tatters drew his umbrella and Grampa looked down the sights of his gun into the flaming throat of Enorma herself. For a moment nothing happened, for the dragon, now that she was down the hill, seemed to wait for them to make the first move.

"Don't shoot," begged the Prince of Ragbad imploringly. "Don't shoot yet Grampa, it's the first time I've been warm to-day!"

Grampa's whiskers had already thawed out and the heat from the fire-breathing monster was so comforting that they almost forgot their fear. The dragon, on her part, seemed more curious than angry.

"Well, I'll be snowballed!" she snorted, wagging her head from side to side. "How did you get here?"

"It's a long strange story," sighed Grampa, lowering his gun and holding his hands toward the waves of heat that blew from the dragon's nostrils.

"We fell, swam, sailed and exploded," crowed Bill, flapping his wings over the dragon's head.

"Well, before you melt, would you mind telling me why you came at all?" asked Enorma, with a terrific yawn.

"Melt!" exclaimed Grampa, his eyes snapping, "why, I'm just beginning to thaw out."

"Well, you'll soon be entirely out of the way," said the dragon comfortably. "The folk hereabout melt at my mere approach." Enorma yawned again and began to pant a little, from her slide down the hill.

"Humph!" grunted the old soldier. At the first yawn he had made a startling discovery—at the second he was sure he had made it. Taking out his snuff box, the old soldier tiptoed close to the monster and flung the entire contents in her face.

Then, "Run for your lives!" shouted Grampa, starting off at his best pace. And it is well that they quickly obeyed this command, for the sneezes of that dragon shook the entire island and sent the snow in blinding flurries all around them.

"What—what's happening?" asked the Prince of Ragbad, peering out wildly from behind an icy cliff.

"Your fortune's made, that's all!" announced Grampa proudly. "More ways than one of winning a battle."

Stepping out, and motioning for the others to follow, the old soldier approached the still quivering monster. Tears streamed from her eyes and she was still sneezing broken-heartedly.

"Enorma is as false as her teeth!" puffed Grampa, and with astonishment Tatters and

Urtha saw that the dragon was perfectly toothless—having lost her one and only set at the first pinch of Grampa's snuff.

"Will you finish her off, or shall I?" asked the old soldier, rattling his sword in businesslike fashion. Before Tatters could answer Enorma gave a frightened moan and began scuttling across the snow fields like an express train bound for Atlantic City.

"Halt! Stop! or I'll fall on your head! Come back here at once and be slaughtered!" screamed Bill, flying after her while the others followed as fast as they could on foot. But in the end Enorma finished herself for, turning to see how close Grampa and Tatters were coming, she plunged headfirst into an icy stream and put herself out—completely and entirely out—for a dragon can no more stand a dash of water than a furnace, or a witch!

When Grampa and Tatters reached the edge of the stream, Enorma was floating like a great green log on the surface, only a tiny puff of smoke to show that she had ever been a roaring, fire-eating, sure-enough monster.

Gentle little Urtha wept a bit but Tatters soon comforted her. Then he and the old soldier moored Enorma fast to a tree, so that they would have proof of their valor when they met the King of the Island. They were all warm

from the encounter with the dragon, but it soon wore off and it wasn't long before they began to shiver again.

"Wish we'd brought one of those house plants along," sighed Tatters.

"Wish I could get my teeth in one of Mrs Sew-and-Sew's ragamuffins," murmured Grampa, trudging gloomily over the snow.

"Bill's found something," called Urtha, who was dancing a few steps ahead. Just then down came the weather cock to announce that he had discovered the dragon's cave. It was tunneled out of a huge, snowy hill and at one end burned a roaring fire. Dragons, as you know, drink flame as other creatures drink water and Enorma always kept a huge pile of trees burning in her cavern.

"Bill, you're a real explorer!" cried Grampa and, taking off one of his medals, he hung it 'round the weather cock's neck. Stacked against the walls of the cave were great piles of frozen meat, for Enorma—in spite of her false teeth—had been a mighty huntress. In a trice Grampa had a bear steak sputtering on the fire on pointed sticks and nothing could have been cozier than their breakfast.

"I told you our troubles were over," beamed the old soldier, handing Tatters a portion of the steak on a tin army plate. "All we have to do now is to claim the reward, find the King's head and journey back to Ragbad." Grampa grinned with satisfaction.

"But how can we do that?" asked Tatters dubiously. "There's the ocean and the sandy desert between."

"Don't worry," advised Grampa, settling comfortably before the fire. "This old Chin Chilly will be so delighted to have the dragon out of the way that he'll probably send us home in a golden ship with our pockets full of

diamonds. How will you like that, Loveliness?"
Urtha was playing hide and seek with Bill but
at Grampa's words she came over to the fire.

"I'll like it if Tatters does," said the little
flower fairy, smiling shyly at the Prince of
Ragbad.

"Well, I'll like it," admitted Tatters, "espe-
cially with *you* along, for we can dance on the
deck and play scrum. Why, I've never had time
to teach you yet. Grampa, won't you lend us
your leg?"

"Not now," objected the old soldier. "Duty
before pleasure, my children. Remember that
we have not found this Chin Chilly, nor claimed
the reward. As we're warmed up and fed we'd
better start hunting again."

"Here I go by the name of Bill," crowed the
weather cock, flinging out of the cavern.
Grampa stowed some of the dried bear meat in
his knapsack and then, forming his little
company in line, gave the order to march away.

"First we'll have another look at the dragon,"
said the old soldier, "and then we'll try to find
the palace of Isa Poso."

So down the snowy hill they marched and
slid and they had just come to the banks of the
stream when harsh voices from the other side
of a clump of trees made them stop short.

"Flowers!" screamed the first voice. "Pull
them up, tread them down! Who dares to plant
flowers on Isa Poso?"

"Foot-prints, too, Chilly dear," grunted a

deeper voice. "Here is an animal with un-matched feet."

Dropping on his knees, the old soldier peered around the frozen tree trunks and saw two of the islanders bending over the tracks they had made when they chased Enorma. They were towering men of snow, with faces of roughly cut ice and so cruel and forbidding in appearance that just to think of them makes me shudder. Fortunately Grampa was not so easily frightened as I am.

"Animals indeed!" spluttered the old soldier. "Company! Forward march!" And Grampa rushed through the trees so fast that Tatters and Urtha had to run to keep up. So suddenly did they burst out upon the little group of islanders that several of the snow men fell over backwards.

"Where is the King?" shouted Grampa, giving his drum such a whack that three more of the company collapsed. But they quickly recovered themselves and, instead of answering, the tallest snow man flung out his arms toward Urtha.

"Stand still!" he commanded angrily. "You're ruining my island. Look at the foolish creature cluttering up the place with flowers!"

Urtha shrank back toward Tatters and the young Prince, speechless with indignation, grasped his umbrella and prepared to attack. But Grampa restrained him and with another resounding whack of his drum strode up to the speaker.

"Is this your island?" asked the old soldier, stamping his game foot.

"Yes, and what are you doing on it?" demanded Chin Chilly, stamping his snow foot. "Just to look at you makes me want to melt!"

"Go ahead and melt," advised Grampa coldly—by this time he was very cold—"but before you do and before you give us any more of your chin music, hand over the reward. I lay claim to half the Kingdom and the Princess in the name of Prince Tatters of Ragbad!"

"Has he slain the dragon?" asked the King, with a gasp of surprise. His manner changed at once and, looking as pleasant as a fellow with icicle whiskers well can, he turned to Tatters. The Prince of Ragbad nodded shortly, for he had not forgotten the King's rudeness to Urtha, and Grampa waved his sword toward the body of Enorma, still floating half in and half out of the water. Running down to the edge of the stream, the snow men began to hug one another and dance up and down with excitement.

"This way! This way!" chuckled Chin Chilly, rubbing his hands together gleefully. Grampa, his head held high and his chest thrust out proudly, followed—for Grampa felt that this was a great day in the history of Ragbad—but Tatters was beginning to have misgivings about the Princess of Isa Poso.

CHAPTER 13

Tatters Receives the Reward

PRINCE TATTERS had little time to think of either the ship or the fortune, for after a short march over the snow, Chin Chilly stepped across a small neck of land and the little army found themselves on a great block of ice, only connected with the island itself by the narrow strip on which they had crossed. A messenger had already been dispatched for the Princess and, standing first on one foot then on the other, Tatters impatiently awaited her approach. Urtha, remembering Chin Chilly's

134

distaste for flowers, kept perfectly still, holding fast to Tatters' coat-tails and peering anxiously in the direction the messenger had taken.

"Just like the old days; just like the old days!" boasted Grampa, stamping up and down to keep warm. But when, a moment later, the Princess of Isa Poso actually appeared, the old soldier nearly fell from under his hat. Yes, really! For the Princenss was a maiden of ice and, wrapped in her robes of snow, she stared at the Prince of Ragbad so frigidly and with such cold and dreadful disdain that a chill ran down his spine and icicles formed on his lashes.

"My boy," stuttered Grampa, rushing over to his side, "I'm afraid we've been a bit hasty. Let us consider this matter a little further."

"None of that," fumed Chin Chilly, bustling forward hastily. "None of that. My word is my word. I insist upon keeping it."

"We'll take your word if you'll keep your daughter," began Grampa quickly. But, advancing with mincing little steps, the icy Princess held out her hand. Her nose was so long and sharp that it made Tatters squint but before he could make any objection she seized his hand in her cold clasp. At the same moment all the snow men except Chin Chilly sprang back across the little neck of land.

"Run!" panted Grampa, tugging Tatters by the coat.

"Run!" gasped Urtha. But before Tatters could run there was a blinding flash. Chin

135

Chilly had raised his sword, snapped off his daughter's hand and, seizing her by the other one, he dragged her back across the strip of land. Then, before a body could wink, the snow men with their sharp axes chopped away this connecting link leaving Grampa and his company marooned on the desolate iceberg.

"You have my daughter's hand, but she's already grown another," shouted Chin Chilly maliciously. And so she had! The little party on the ice could plainly see that for themselves. "You have my daughter's hand and *that* is your half of the Kingdom," shrieked the wretched old snow King, nearly bending double at his own joke.

"Half the Kingdom and the Princess' hand!" snorted the old soldier in a fury. "I'll snap off his whiskers! I'll pound him to snow flakes!"

Gathering himself together, Grampa prepared to jump back to Isa Poso. But Tatters, flinging the hand of the Princess as far as he could, seized Grampa around the waist. And it is well that he did, for already there was a great stretch of tumbling waters between the iceberg and the island.

"He has no more honor than a sword-fish!" spluttered Grampa, breaking away from the Prince. "I've never been so insulted in my life!"

"Where is the golden ship?" demanded an indignant voice. "Where are the diamonds? What have you done with the Princess?"

Dropping with a thud that sent a shower of

ice splinters into the air, the weather cock planted himself before Grampa. He had been looking all over Isa Poso for Chin Chilly and had arrived just in time to see his friends sailing off on the iceberg.

"Oh, Bill!" cried Urtha, giving the iron bird an impulsive hug, "I thought you were lost!"

"Where is the golden ship? Where are the diamonds?" insisted the weather cock, slipping out of Urtha's embrace.

"Oh, go crack yourself some icicles," muttered the old soldier crossly. He did not like to be reminded of his cheerful prophecy. "Go crack yourself some icicles, Bill, that's all the diamonds you'll get."

"There isn't any ship—nor any diamonds— nor anything!" said Tatters, wrapping the skin of the old thread bear more tightly about him and staring drearily over the tossing waters of the Nonestic Ocean.

"But you don't have to marry the Princess," Urtha reminded him softly, "and even if this isn't a golden ship couldn't we dance and be happy?"

"Well, if we don't dance, we'll freeze," fumed Grampa, beginning to stamp up and down. "We'll freeze anyway," he predicted gloomily. "Look pleasant, my boy. We might as well freeze as attractively as possible. They'll carve us a monument on a block of ice, no doubt: 'Frozen in the line of duty!'"

Tatters coughed plaintively and began to tramp sadly up and down after Grampa.

"Don't freeze," begged the little flower fairy, clasping her hands in distress and keeping step with the down-hearted adventurers. "Why, where's that funny bottle?" she asked suddenly.

"The medicine! What have you done with the wizard's medicine?" crowed the weather cock, flapping his wings. Now so much had happened to the old soldier since the eruption that he had entirely forgotten Gorba's cure for everything. But at Urtha's words he snatched it out and, there, listed under colds, chills, frost bites and exposure, Grampa found a remedy for their troubles.

"You've saved our lives, my dear," sighed the old soldier, measuring out four drops for Tatters on a spoonful of snow. And everything was better after that, for as soon as Grampa and the Prince swallowed the marvelous mixture they began to tingle with warmth and even an iceberg could not long be cheerless with a little fairy like Urtha aboard. Everywhere she stepped gay posies blossomed and soon there were circles and circles of them bobbing in the bright sunshine. Urtha and Bill did not feel the cold, and as Grampa and Tatters were now frost proof, their whole outlook changed. The huge iceberg was sliding along through the choppy waves at high speed and the sensation was not only pleasant but highly exhilarating.

"Which way are we going?" asked the old soldier, sitting down recklessly on a cake of ice.

"East," announced the weather cock, after twirling around three times like a top.

"That's good," sighed Grampa, "for East of us lies Oz and the nearer we come to Oz, the farther we get from Isa Poso."

"I never want to see it again! And if that is a sample of your Princesses, I'll be like you, Grampa, and never marry," said the Prince, taking a seat beside the old soldier. "I think, myself, that if we can find my father's head, we'd better just go home anyway. We could work hard in the gingham gardens, raise bigger crops and—"

"And I'll help you," smiled Urtha, drifting about over the ice like an old-fashioned bouquet and filling the frosty air with a lovely fragrance.

"But the fortune," objected Bill, staring at

the Prince in horror. "We have to find the fortune."

"That's right," agreed the old soldier, remembering Mrs Sew-and-Sew's words about refurnishing the castle. "We mustn't give up yet, just because we've bumped into some odd and chilly places. Just wait—there are lots of Princesses in Oz, and fortunes too!"

"Well I prefer fairies," sighed Tatters, with a smile at Urtha.

"Look!" cried the little flower girl delightedly. "Let's pretend this is a silver ship and there—" as a spray of crystal drops dashed over the side of the iceberg—"there are the diamonds! Let's dance!" She looked so coaxing and so cunning that Tatters sprang up impulsively and the two went skipping, sliding and twirling all over the ice until they were dancing on a perfect carpet of flowers.

"Teach her the Ragbad quadrille," called Grampa. "If we're going back with a fortune, there'll be high old times in the red castle and Urtha will want to know the dances the same as the other girls. Wait, I'll play it for you."

Seizing his drum sticks, the old soldier broke into the spirited measures of the Ragbad quadrille and soon Tatters and Urtha were bowing and gliding, turning three times to the left and four to the right, pretending to change partners with a dozen imaginary courtiers—all troubles and dangers forgotten.

"This reminds me of old times," said Grampa,

stopping at last from lack of breath. "And you'll never be a wall-flower, my dear!" chuckled the old soldier, wagging his finger at the little fairy.

"Let's play scrum," proposed Tatters, who was perfectly breathless too.

"Oh let's!" cried Urtha. So Grampa obligingly unfastened his game leg, and the Prince and little flower girl were soon deep in the mysteries of the queer old game of scrum, Bill keeping score on the ice and the old soldier, with half closed eyes, thinking of the good old days when he was a lad and a hero to all the pretty girls in Ragbad.

"First peaceful moment we've had since we left the old country," mused Grampa and, reaching down, he picked up his pipe and tobacco. Tatters had removed them from the game leg before they started to play. Absently Grampa filled his pipe from one of the pouches—the blue pouch he had taken from Vaga, the bandit. All this time it had lain forgotten in Grampa's game leg. Without realizing that he had used the robber's tobacco, Grampa felt for a match. At the same moment Urtha and Tatters finished their fifth game of scrum and, closing up the game leg, they buckled it back in place.

"Now tell me all about Ragbad," begged Urtha, leaning against Grampa's knee. This Tatters was only too delighted to do, for the young Prince was heartily homesick and, as he could not be in Ragbad, talking about it was

141

the next best thing. So he told little Urtha all
about his pigeons and the Redsmith and Pudge's
tower—where you could see clear out into
Jinxland—and of the fun he and Grampa had
in the old castle and of Mrs Sew-and-Sew's
garden. The old soldier nodded from time to
time and at last, taking up his pipe, he began
to smoke. I say began, for at the third puff a
simply astonishing thing happened. Bill van-
ished instanter [and you know how quick that
is]. Tatters turned to a great black crow, Urtha
to a crow of vari-colored feathers, and Grampa,
himself, to an old crow with a game leg.

"Help!" cawed the old soldier, dropping the
pipe from his bill and beginning to hop wildly
over the ice.

"Daisies and dahlias, I can fly!" twittered
Urtha, circling aloft. "Come on Tatters and try
it!"

142

"He's a crow!" shrieked Grampa. "I'm a crow, you're a crow! What's happened and where's Bill?"

"Here I am," screamed a frightened voice. But though they stared and stared they could see nothing at all—for Bill had turned to a cock's crow, which of course can only be heard and not seen.

"Poor Bill, there's nothing left but his crow," cawed Grampa.

"It's magic," gasped Tatters.

"It's that pesky wizard," added the old soldier, stamping his game foot and ruffling up all his feathers, for Grampa did not realize he'd smoked Vaga's tobacco.

"But now that we're crows why not fly?" asked Urtha merrily. She did not seem to mind her feathers at all. "Let's fly back to Oz!"

"Why, so we can!" cried Tatters. "All the way over the Nonestic Ocean and sandy desert, straight to the Emerald City itself. Someone's helping us, Grampa," finished the Prince of Ragbad, fluttering into the air.

"Wish they'd mind their own business," croaked Grampa crossly. "Being a crow is no help to me. But come on. We might as well fly while we can. Bill, you lead the way and see that you keep us pointed East and crow every few minutes, will you, so we can hear where you are."

"All right," agreed the weather cock readily, and they could tell from the flutter of his iron wings that the puzzled bird had gotten under way.

"Here I go by the name of Bill!" he crowed loudly.

"Invisi-Bill!" chortled the old soldier, rising into the air. "Come on crows!"

Tatters quickly followed Grampa and after Tatters flew Urtha, higher and higher and higher, until the iceberg became only a tiny speck, bobbing up and down in the blue waters of the Nonestic Ocean.

For a time the adventurers flew in silence, each one pondering the strange events that had crowded upon them in the past few hours. "Invisi-Bill" continued to lead the way, Grampa, Prince Tatters and Urtha winging after him.

CHAPTER 14

On Monday Mountain

"GOOD SLEEP, how did you enjoy your morning?" asked Percy Vere brightly.

"Pretty well," smiled Dorothy, sitting up with a little yawn. "How did you enjoy your sleep?"

"There was a rock in my bed," said the Forgetful Poet thoughtfully, "and then I got trying to think of a word to rhyme with schnetzel."

"How about pretzel?" suggested Dorothy, smiling a little to herself at the Forgetful Poet's earnestness. "And what is a schnetzel?" Dorothy smiled sweetly.

"It's a green mocking bird," explained Percy Vere, tossing back his hair, "and it does live on pretzels. My dear, you have a wonderful mind."

"Woof!" interrupted Toto. He had been up for hours and wanted his breakfast. The three travellers had been forced to spend the night in the deep forest to which the runaway had brought them. The Forgetful Poet had piled up a soft couch of boughs and leaves for Dorothy and Toto, but had flung himself carelessly under a tree. However, it took more than a hard bed to dash Percy's spirits and, after running up and down a few paces to get the stiffness out of his bones, he began to sing at the top of his voice, filling in the words he forgot with such comical made-up ones that Dorothy could not help laughing.

"I think we are going to have a lucky day, Mr. Vere," said the little girl, hopping up merrily. "Don't you?"

Percy, who was washing his face in a nearby brook, nodded so vigorously that the water splashed in every direction.

"I should say!—April, May!" he called gaily.

"Why do you put in April May?" asked Dorothy, running over to splash her own hands in the brook.

"To keep in practice," puffed the Forgetful

Poet. "Is that plain—aeroplane? Is that clear—summer's here? I'm always afraid I shall run out of rhymes," confided Percy, drying his face on his yellow silk handkerchief. "So when I'm talking in prose, I usually add a line under my breath."

"Oh!" said Dorothy, and lowered her head so that the Forgetful Poet would not see her smile. "You'll like Scraps," observed Dorothy presently. "She's a poet too." And as they walked through the fragrant forest, Dorothy told him all about the Patch Work Girl, who lives in the Emerald City. Scraps, as most of you know, is one of the most famous characters in Oz, being entirely made from a patch work quilt and magically brought to life.

"Does she make better verses than I do?" asked Percy jealously.

"No," answered Dorothy, shaking her head, "not any better, and yours are such fun to finish." This speech so tickled Percy Vere that he recited a verse upon the spot, waving his arms so ferociously that Toto hid under a rock. The little dog peered out from his hiding place to hear the strange young poet deliver this jingle—which his little doggie head could not comprehend in the slightest:

> "As I came out of Snoozleburg,
>   I met a melon collie;
> He wept because he said he felt
>   So terribly unjolly!

147

"I patted him upon the head;
  He bit me on the shin—
Which goes to show just what
  A horrid temper he was—was—"

"In," giggled Dorothy, "and did he really?"

"No, unreally," chuckled the Forgetful Poet, leaning down to give Toto's ear an afectionate little tweak. "Unreally! Unreally! Unreally! As unreally as the breakfast we had this morning. Dorothy, my dear, I'm as weak as tea!"

"Well, you don't look it," laughed the little girl mischievously. "But I see a hut between those two pines. Perhaps someone lives there."

"Tut tut! A hut;
  Let's hasten to it!
If the door is shut
  I'll jump right—?"

"All right!" said Dorothy merrily. "C'mon!"

The door was shut but when the Forgetful Poet turned the knob it opened easily and they found themselves in a small, simply furnished cabin. There was no one home, but there were eggs, coffee, bacon and bread in the cupboard, so Percy made a fire in the little stove and Dorothy quickly prepared an appetizing breakfast.

"It must belong to a woodcutter," said Dorothy as they sat down cozily together, "and I don't believe he'll mind."

"I'll leave a poem to pay for it," said Percy loftily.

"And I'll leave my ring," added Dorothy. She was a little afraid the woodcutter might not appreciate Percy's poem.

While Dorothy washed up the dishes Percy scribbled away busily on some sheets of paper he had found on the table and, after a good many corrections, he pinned the following verse up on the wall:

"We've eaten up a little bacon
And eggs and such and now are takin'
Our leave. Accept our thanks, and you
Should feel a little honored to
Have entertained with humble fare
A really celebrated pair—
A Princess and a Poet, who
Wish you good-luck, good-day, a—"

Dorothy took the pencil and added a large dieu to Percy's last line. Then, leaving her gold ring on the table, she skipped after the Forgetful Poet and Toto, who were already out of doors and anxious to be off.

"Which way shall we go?" Dorothy paused a moment. "I think the Emerald City is in this direction," she decided at last, facing toward the West.

"Well, I hope so," sighed Percy Vere, "for otherwise we shall never find the Princess. I wish I'd flung that prophet out of the window— so I do!" You see the young poet was getting very much discouraged.

"But even if you had, there still would be the monster to think about," Dorothy reminded him. "And if she's lost from us, she's lost from the monster, too!"

"That's so," said the Forgetful Poet, cheering up immediately. "You think of everything, don't you. I'm going to write a book of verse about you when I get back to Perhaps City."

"That'll be nice," smiled Dorothy. "But let's hurry up and see how far we can be by noon-time." And hurry up it certainly was, for the path Dorothy had chosen grew steeper and steeper. It wound in and out among the trees and was so rough and full of stones that they had to stop every once in a while to rest.

"It's a mountain—go fountain!" panted Percy Vere, after they had toiled steadily upward for more than an hour.

"Never mind," puffed Dorothy, tucking Toto under her arm—for the poor bow-bow was completely worn out—"when we reach the top we'll know where we are."

The trees had thinned out by this time and clouds of vapor hid the top of the mountain from view, but Dorothy and the Forgetful Poet kept climbing upward—on and on and up.

"It's a dreadful blue mountain," said Dorothy at last, leaning against a rock.

"It's blue as blueing," groaned Percy Vere, shaking a stone out of his shoe. "What's this?"

"What's that?" cried Dorothy, in the same breath. Now this—as it happened—was a clothes horse, full of petticoats and pajamas—and as the two travellers stared at it in disbelief it kicked up its pegs and dashed off at a gallop, its petticoats and pajamas snapping in the breeze. And that was a wash woman—a wild, wild wash woman, her hair dragged up on top of her head and held in place by a couple of clothes pins. She had a clothes prop in one hand and a cake of soap in the other. Hurling both with all her might at Percy Vere, she turned and scrambled up the mountain, screaming in a dozen different keys as she scrambled. The clothes prop missed, but the great cake of soap caught Percy squarely in the stomach.

"Ugh!" grunted the Forgetful Poet, sitting down from the shock:

> "How rude, how rough, how awfully waste-
> ful—
> The lady's manners are dis—dis—?"

"Gusting," panted Dorothy—who was too frightened to make a rhyme.

"Can you fight?" she asked breathlessly, helping Percy to his feet. "I think there's going to be a fight. Look!"

Percy snatched up the cake of soap that had felled him and turned to see what was coming. Through the clouds of steam that hung over the mountain top there suddenly burst a terrible company.

Toto hid his head in Dorothy's blouse and the Forgetful Poet could think of no verse to express his feelings. No wonder! A charge of wild wash women is enough to frighten the bravest traveller and that is exactly what was coming. An army of wash women armed with long bars of soap, bottles of blueing, clothes props, wash boards, tubs and baskets. They were huge and fat, with rolled-up sleeves and cross, red faces, and the faster they ran the crosser they grew, and the crosser they grew the faster they ran.

"Doesn't seem polite to fight the ladies, but—" Percy raised his arm and flung the cake with all his might at the head of the advancing army. It struck her smartly on the nose and, with a howl of rage, she dropped her wash tub and rushed upon the two helpless adventurers.

"Wash their faces! Iron their hands and wring their necks!" she roared hoarsely.

"What are you doing here you—you—scutter-mullions!"

Before either could answer, and Percy was racking his brains to think of a word to rhyme with scutter-mullions, she had Dorothy by one arm and the Forgetful Poet by the other, shaking them until they couldn't have spoken had they tried—while the others pressed so close (as Dorothy told Ozma afterwards) it's a wonder they weren't smothered on the spot. But at last, weary of shaking them, the wild wash woman flung them down upon a rock.

"You're a disgrace to our mountain!" she panted angrily. "Look at your clothes!" (To be quite truthful Dorothy and the Forgetful Poet were looking shabby and dusty in the extreme.)

"Give me his coat! Give me her dress! Snatch off their socks!" screamed the other wash women, making little snatches at the two on the rock.

Percy put his arms protectingly around Dorothy and Toto showed all his teeth and began to growl so terribly that even the head of the wash women stepped back.

"What are you doing on Monday Mountain?" she demanded indignantly.

"Monday Mountain?" gasped Percy Vere. "Did you hear that, Dorothy? We're on Monday Mountain! Great blueing, black and blueing!" finished Percy, with a groan.

"Stop mumbling and speak up!" shouted the wash woman threateningly.

"Stop shouting and shut up!" barked Toto unexpectedly.

"We're searching for a Princess," explained Dorothy, in the surprised silence that followed Toto's remark.

"A Princess! Oh, mother!"

Out from the dreadful group sprang a perfectly enormous wash girl.

"Tell them, tell them!" She gave the leader of the tribe a playful push. "Oh, mother, may I have him?"

"My daughter is a Princess," announced the wash woman grandly, "Princess of the Tubbies, and as this yellow bird pleases her he may remain."

"And marry me?' exulted the Princess of

Monday Mountain, clasping her fat hands in glee.

"Marry you!" shouted Percy Vere, springing to his feet. "Never! Absolutely no—domi-no!

Dorothy, Dorothy, do you hear what they are saying?"

Dorothy did not, for she had both hands over her ears. The shouts and screams of the Tubbies, at Percy's refusal to marry their Princess, were so shrill and piercing that she thought her head would split with the racket.

"To the wash tubs with them!" screamed the Queen furiously. "Wash their faces, wring their necks, hang them up to dry!"

And, seizing upon the luckless pair, the wild wash women bore them struggling and kicking to the top of Monday Mountain—Toto dashing after—and the herds of clothes horses that graze on the mountain side scattering in every direction as they passed.

CHAPTER 15

The Finding of Fumbo's Head!

FOR AN HOUR the three crows and Invisi-Bill flew steadily over the Nonestic Ocean, and flying was so unusual and pleasant a sensation that they were too interested to talk. Besides, Grampa had warned them in the beginning to keep all their strength for flying, for there was no telling how long they would remain crows and it would be extremely dangerous to change back while up in the air and over the ocean. So, except for the occasional calls of Bill to let them know which way to go, they crossed the great ocean in silence.

157

"Land!" screamed the weather cock, as the rocky shores of Ev came into view.

"Well, that's over!" cawed Grampa, alighting thankfully on a rough cliff. "Now we must cross this country and the sandy desert. Anybody tired?"

Urtha and Tatters shook their heads and no one could see what Bill did, so after a few minutes' rest they rose into the air again and flew swiftly over Ev—on and on until they reached the great desert that entirely surrounds the magic Kingdom of Oz.

"Fly higher!" commanded the old soldier, for he had read so much of the deadly nature of this desert that he wanted to be as far above it as possible. So the little flock of crows and Invisi-Bill soared high into the air and they crossed the desert even faster than they had crossed the Nonestic Ocean, fear lending speed to their wings. And when at last the lovely land of the Winkies spread out below them, the old soldier gave a crow of delight. "Just keep on this way and we'll be in the Emerald City by noon time!" exulted Grampa. "Forward for Ragbad and Oz!"

"And flying is such fun," chuckled Urtha, circling close to the old soldier. "I don't care how long I am a crow. But, oh Mr Grampa, there's a gun sticking through your feathers."

"What?" croaked the old soldier in alarm.

"I feel heavy," spluttered Tatters suddenly, and looking at the young Prince, Grampa saw

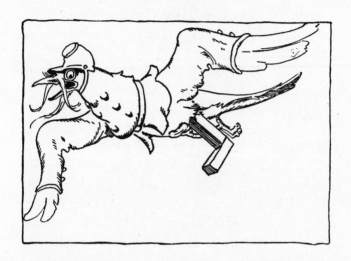

that from the waist down he was Tatters and from the waist up he still was crow.

"Down! Everybody down! Down as fast as you can fly," ordered the old soldier in a panic. He himself could feel his feathers turning to clothes and his wings seemed too light to hold up his body. Half flying and half falling, half people and half crows, the little company shot downward, and it is mighty lucky they started down when they did. As it was, they turned back to themselves and landed at one and the same minute, and the landing was so hard that, for a moment, no one spoke at all. The old soldier broke the silence.

"Why, there's Bill," cried Grampa, who was sitting calmly in the middle of a yellow rose bush. He had grown somewhat used to falling

159

about by this time. "How do you feel, Bill?" asked the old soldier, extracting several thorns from his person.

"How do I look?" asked the weather cock anxiously.

"Handsome as ever," said Grampa, eying him closely. "Being invisible hasn't hurt you at all, and how are the rest of my old cronies?"

"I'm all right," smiled Urtha, jumping up lightly. The little flower maiden was looking as beautiful as ever.

"So am I," said Tatters, "but I'd like to know how we happened to turn crow, and whether it's going to happen often. You know, Grampa, it would be mighty inconvenient to be turning backwards and forwards any minute. I am sure it would be very unpleasant."

"Well, it helped us over a couple of bad places," mused the old soldier. "The mischief, boys! I've lost my pipe!" Grampa clapped one hand to his pocket and the other to his chin.

"You dropped it when you were a crow," Tatters reminded him. Grampa did not answer, for out of his pocket he had drawn the blue tobacco pouch of Vaga, the bandit. In the excitement following Bill's disappearance all the tobacco had spilled out, but the pouch Grampa had thrust into his pocket just before he turned crow. Here, at any rate, it was, and on the flap this amazing sentence: "To turn people to crows, smoke this tobacco. One puff will keep a company of captives crows for one hour, two puffs, two hours, three puffs for three hours, and so on."

"So that's the reason there were so many crows in the blue forest!" shouted Grampa indignantly. "So that's why we turned to crows. It's three hours to the minute," he puffed, pulling out his watch.

"What *are* you talking about?" asked Tatters crossly.

"Us," chuckled Grampa. "It was the bandit's tobacco that did the trick." Showing them the blue pouch, he explained how he had smoked the magic tobacco instead of his own and how just three puffs had kept them crows for three hours. "A couple more puffs and we'd have been all the way to the Emerald City," sighed the old soldier regretfully. "How-some-ever, marching is more to my taste."

"What about eating? That's more to mine." Tatters yawned—for flying had made him quite hungry.

"All right," agreed Grampa, and, unfastening his knapsack, he took out one of the dried bear steaks and busied himself with making a fire. Fortunately they had lost none of their possessions by turning to crows—that is nothing except Grampa's pipe.

"I love this country," said Urtha, sitting solemnly beside the old soldier. "I believe I like Oz better than the wizard's garden."

"It's the top of the world," boasted Grampa, dropping the steak into his campaign frying pan. Tatters, meanwhile, had found a pink plum tree and came back with his cap full of plums, so that he and Grampa had a most satisfying luncheon. Bill, as usual, was searching for the fortune and, while they were eating, Urtha merrily skipped rope with a long spray of honeysuckle.

"Cheer up, boy," said the old soldier, for the Prince was looking rather thoughtful. "We're on the right track now and only a day's march from the capitol."

"Storm coming! Storm coming!" shrilled the weather cock, dropping down suddenly beside the fire. "Wind! Thunder and possible showers!"

"Oh, g'wan!" scoffed Grampa, gathering up his tin camp dishes. "You g'wan, Bill."

"I don't want to go on," said the weather cock stubbornly. "There's a storm coming, I tell you." And sure enough, at that minute, a great gust of wind scattered the camp fire, blew off Grampa's hat and sent a cloud of leaves scurrying over the meadows. Tatters reached for his red umbrella, which was never far from his side and Urtha, her flowery skirts flying out like ribbons on a May pole, came hurrying back.

"I've thought of something!" screamed Bill. He had to scream to make himself heard, for the wind had risen to a perfect gale. "If the

162

King's head was lost in a storm, why wouldn't it be found in a storm!"

"Snuff and nonsense!" shouted the old soldier, picking up his hat and jamming it over his ears. Then, as the first spatter of rain came pelting down, he dashed under the big red umbrella. Tatters had all he could do to hold it steady and several times the wind nearly jerked him into the air. So Grampa seized the handle with both hands and Urtha, also, took hold. But it was no use. The gale was too much for them and before they had time to let go, the red umbrella whirled up like a balloon, carrying them all along.

"Here I come by the name of Bill!" shrieked the weather cock and, flinging himself aloft, he scrambled on top of the King's umbrella. But even Bill's weight could not bring it down.

"Why this," laughed the little flower fairy, as the umbrella soared up toward the clouds, "this is better than flying!"

"Better hold on," advised Grampa grimly, "there's nothing between us and earth, but air." The wind rose higher and higher, the rain swirled all around them and tossed them about like rag dolls. The three clung desperately to the umbrella but in ten minutes they had risen above the storm area and were sailing straight toward a great patch of pink skyland. About halfway over, the umbrella drifted slowly downward and Grampa and Tatters, rather uncertainly, stood up in the pink clouds.

"Will we drop through?" asked the Prince doubtfully, still keeping hold of the umbrella. After a few steps they found it quite as secure as the real earth.

"How soft it feels," murmured Urtha and, letting go of the umbrella, she began skipping over the fluffy cloud meadows, posies springing up wherever she stepped, just as they had on Isa Poso. And so fresh and beautiful did the little flower girl appear against the pink of the clouds that Grampa and Tatters simply gasped

and a little sky shepherdess, who had been resting on a cloud bank, picked up her crook and came running over to touch Urtha.

"Are you a fairy?" asked the little shepherdess breathlessly.

"Are you a Princess?" demanded Bill, fluttering down in front of the little sky lady before Urtha had time to speak at all. Bill never allowed anything to interfere with business.

"Oh, no!" The cunning little lady swung her moon bonnet and fluffed out her skirts, which were all embroidered with stars. "Oh, no, I'm only a shepherdess!" she answered modestly.

"Well, we're looking for a head, a Princess and a fortune," rasped Bill impatiently.

"What do you shepherd?" asked the old soldier, pushing Bill hurriedly aside. "I didn't know there were any sheep in the sky."

"Not sheep," cried the little maiden, throwing back her head and laughing heartily, "not sheep, but stars! I tend all the baby stars and keep them from falling out of the Milky Way," she finished, smiling shyly at Tatters.

"You do," marvelled the Prince of Ragbad, "well, where are they now and what do you call yourself?"

"I never call myself, but the stars call me Maribella," answered the little shepherdess, with a demure bow. "They're asleep now. Are you *really* looking for a Princess?"

Tatters nodded and Urtha, slipping her arms around Maribella's waist, kissed her on both cheeks.

"I wish you were the Princess," sighed Urtha, stepping back to look wistfully at the little sky maiden.

"Why?" asked Maribella curiously.

"Because you're the only one we've seen who

is lovely enough to marry the Prince," said Urtha. Tatters looked mightily embarrassed at Urtha's speech and Grampa, drawing Maribella aside told her the whole story of their adventures.

"Well," mused the little sky maiden as he finished, "there aren't any Princesses or fortunes in the sky, but there are lots of heads here in the clouds."

"There are!" roared Grampa in astonishment. Maribella nodded.

"Didn't you know many earth people have their heads in the clouds?" she asked seriously. "Why there's a whole company of them on the other side of this very hill."

"Forward, march!" cried the old soldier excitedly. "Urtha, Tatters, Bill, fall in with you!" So fall in they did, and Maribella was right, for on the other side of the cloud hill were nearly a hundred heads, resting lightly on the pink clouds. Some were smoking, some stared straight ahead and others were carrying on a lively conversation between themselves.

"Father!" screamed the Prince of Ragbad, for King Fumbo's head was almost the first they spied. Fumbo was talking quietly to the head of an inventor of market baskets with legs and he turned in some surprise at Tatters' call.

"The head! The head! We have found the head!" crowed Bill exultantly, and burst into such a hurrah of cock-a-doodle-doos that several of the smokers dropped their pipes and King Fumbo looked positively frightened.

"Your Majesty," said Grampa reproachfully, as Bill finally subsided, "how could you leave us like this? We've been through earth, air, fire and water to find you."

"Well, I guess the jig's up," sighed Fumbo sorrowfully, "but it's been a great treat, Grampa, getting off like this. How's everybody?"

"Everybody was well enough when I left," said Grampa a bit stiffly, for he couldn't help feeling that Fumbo could have got home if he had wanted to. "Everybody's well enough, except your own body and that looks mighty silly with the doughnut they have given it."

"So they gave me a dough head! Well, won't that do?" asked the King fretfully of the old soldier.

"Oh, father, please come back," begged Tatters, falling on his knees before the King's head.

"You must certainly resume your body," declared the old soldier sternly. "How did you get up here in the first place?"

"It was the storm," began Fumbo, rolling his eyes from one to the other. "My head never was on very tight, you know."

Grampa nodded dryly. "So it blew off," continued the King calmly, "and then I had on a wing collar," Fumbo coughed apologetically, "and the thing flew right well, so I flew till I

167

came to this cloud and here I've been ever since. I suppose I must go back if you say so, but it's a poor business, old fellow. How are you going to get down from here? How did you get up? Who is this little Miss Rosy Posy and that iron billed bird you have with you?"

"This is Urtha," explained Tatters proudly. "We found her in an enchanted garden. And that's Bill. We found him in the blue forest and—oh, father, we've had such strange adventures."

"Tell me all!" sighed Fumbo, closing his eyes and smacking his lips with anticipation.

"Not unless you come back with us," said Grampa craftily.

"We were in an island of fire," began Tatters, while Urtha, who was pressed close at his side, nodded excitedly.

"What!" exclaimed Fumbo, opening his eyes as far as they would go. "I'll come!" he decided hastily, "and you must tell me every single bit of the story."

Grampa smiled slyly, Tatters promised and before he could change his mind, the old soldier thrust the King's head into the pink bag Maribella had used for her knitting. Then, accompanied by the little sky shepherdess, Grampa and his army prepared to leave the sky. The other heads looked very sulky as they passed by but, paying no attention to their mutterings, Grampa marched to the edge of the great pink cloud.

"Now what?" mused the old soldier, staring down anxiously. "Are there any steps or air ships about, my dear?"

Maribella shook her head. "But there's a rainbow," she cried suddenly. "Could you use that?" Arching from the edge of the cloud and down as far as they could see, curved a wide glittering rainbow—for the storm was over and the sun was shining through the clouds. Dancing down the rainbow came a fairy almost as lovely as Urtha herself. It was Polychrome, the Rain King's daughter, and when Maribella explained that Grampa and his company were from Oz, she insisted upon kissing them all— for Polychrome had visited in Oz many times and had met with some fine adventures there.

"Come on," cried Polychrome gaily, "I'll show you how to travel on a rainbow." Seizing

Urtha by the hand, she began running down the bow as you and I would run down steps. Calling good-bye to Maribella, Grampa and Tatters quickly followed, the Prince carrying his father's head and the red umbrella and Grampa balancing Bill upon his shoulder.

"Now all we have to find is the Princess and the fortune, and a couple of new pipes," sighed Grampa.

"Ah, let's go home without them," begged Tatters eagerly. "I want to show Urtha the castle and the pigeons. We don't need a fortune to be happy, Grampa."

"Now don't give up yet," advised Grampa, turning to wag his finger at the Prince. "There's always a fortune at the end of the rainbow. Look! I believe we're coming down in the Winkie country, and when we do," Grampa pulled his whiskers determinedly, "I'm going to get myself an anchor. I'm tired of this flying and falling about."

"Use me," crowed Bill, but as he spoke the bow grew suddenly so very slant that instead of running they began to slide—faster and faster and faster.

"Good-bye," called Polychrome mischievously. "I'd come with you, but it's my Daddy's birthday and we're having a party in the sky."

Just as Polly came to "party," Grampa and his army came to the end of the rainbow and tumbled off in fine style. None of them was hurt in the tumble, and all scrambled to their feet as quickly as they could.

"Good-bye, Polychrome," called Urtha. She was the only one who had breath enough to speak.

"Good gracious," puffed the old soldier, "I hope we've not broken your father's head."

"Well, if it's not broken it's badly cracked," raged the King stuffily, from the inside of the bag. "If you're going to fling me about like this I'll not stick with you, do you hear?"

The adventurers smiled and silently put their fingers to their lips, and King Fumbo decided that further protest was useless.

CHAPTER 16

Princess Dorothy Escapes

THE TWO DAYS that Grampa and his little army had been adventuring in the wizard's garden, on Fire Island and Isa Poso, Dorothy, Toto and the Forgetful Poet had spent as prisoners on Monday Mountain. Only the friendship of Princess Pearl Borax had saved them from actual harm, for the Queen of the Tubbies had nearly carried out her threat of wringing their necks. But the Queen finally had sentenced them to the wash tubs, and from morning till night Dorothy and Percy Vere had

172

been forced to bend over the wash boards with the rest of the wild wash women tribe.

Several times during the first day Percy Vere had almost agreed to marry the dreadful daughter of the old wash woman, for he could not bear to see dear little Dorothy working like a slave. The Forgetful Poet himself had never done any hard work, and in an hour he had rubbed all the skin from his knuckles and all the buttons from the clothes. But Dorothy would not hear of his marrying Pearl Borax, so, hiding his own discomfort, Percy did the best he could to keep her cheerful, reciting his ridiculous rhymes and waving the shirts, stockings and pantaloons around his head whenever the Queen's back was turned. Even so, keeping cheerful was hard work and often both grew downhearted.

"And Ozma thinks I'm having a fine visit with the Tin Woodman," sighed Dorothy wearily, toward the end of the second day.

"And Peer Haps thinks I'm rescuing his daughter," groaned Percy Vere, letting the Queen's red table cloth slip back into his tub and staring mournfully down Monday Mountain. Then seeing that Dorothy was actually near to tears, he tilted his cap over one eye and whispered this verse into her right ear:

> "It's wash, splosh, rub
>   And hang 'em up for dryin',
> If sumpin doesn't happen soon
>   I'll simply bust out—?"

"Cryin'!" Dorothy smiled and dashed the tears out of her eyes. "Here comes the old lady!" she finished hurriedly.

"Isn't she simply sinoobious," sniffed Percy, dousing the red table cloth up and down in the water.

"What did you say?" roared the Queen of the Tubbies.

"I said," grinned Percy mischievously:

> "Her Highness is so beautiful
>   Her brightness dims the eye,
> I'll work here and be dutiful
>   Until the day I, I—?"

"Die!" spluttered Dorothy, and the clumsy Queen lumbered on with a pleased smirk.

"Better make up your mind to marry Pearl," she called over her shoulder and Pearl Borax blew Percy a wet kiss over her tub of clothes. Toto, who was tied to Dorothy's tub, growled fiercely—for he loathed the whole tribe of sloppy, messy wash women.

"We must think of a way out," gasped the poor poet unhappily, for life on Monday Mountain, where every day is wash-day, and every dinner is of potatoes and cabbage, was not to be endured. They had been over the matter a hundred times before and there really seemed no chance of escape at all. The tubs of the tribe were ranged in a circle around the mountain top, so that Dorothy and the Forgetful Poet were always under guard. A white fence

ran around the mountain, a few feet below.
You may have heard of a fence running around
before, but this was the first fence Dorothy
every had seen that actually did run. It was
tall and spiked and flashed 'round and 'round,
till just watching it gave one the headache. It
was too high to jump and the gate only came
opposite Dorothy and the Forgetful Poet once
a day.

When they had been dragged up the mountain, the Queen had addressed a low word to
the fence. Immediately it had stopped and they
had all come through the gate. But what *was*
the word? Ever since his capture Percy Vere
had been trying to puzzle it out and now,
leaning his elbows on his wash board, he began
trying again. Indeed he thought until he had
twelve wrinkles in his forehead and all at once,
like a flash of lightning, it came to him—such
a short, sensible word that he gave a triumphant
skip. Next instant he was splashing the clothes
in his tub so vigorously that none of the wild
wash women heard him give Dorothy a few
quick instructions. In five minutes the gate
would be opposite and one minute before the
five were up, the three prisoners dashed down
the mountain.

"Stop!" shouted Percy Vere, imperiously
hammering upon the fence with a rock. Oh,
joy! It did stop and, as the gate was now exactly
in front of them, Percy Vere opened it boldly
and pulled Dorothy and Toto through. No

sooner were they out than the fence began to spin around as fast as ever, so that before the wild wash women, who saw them escape, could follow the gate was half way around the mountain. With howls of rage and fright—for the Tubbies knew that the Queen would be furious—the dreadful creatures overturned their wash tubs, and a perfect torrent of hot soapy water came cascading down the mountain side, upsetting Dorothy and the Forgetful Poet and making the path so slippery that they never stopped sliding till they reached the bottom. Breathless, drenched and shaken, but otherwise unhurt, they picked themselves up and, without pausing to rest, all three began running as fast as ever they could away from Monday Mountain.

"How—did—you—ever—think—of—telling the fence to stop?" puffed Dorothy, stopping under a broad tulip tree.

"Had to!" gasped Percy, dropping heavily to the ground and leaning over to pat Toto, who sat, with closed eyes and tongue out, trying to catch up with his breath. Then Percy delivered this gem:

> "Far from the Tubbies, little Princess,
> And wouldn't they starch and blue and rinse
> us—"

"Did you say Princess?" interrupted a voice. Dorothy and Percy both jumped and Toto gave a frightened bark—for sitting on a lower branch of the tulip tree was our old friend Bill.

"Did you say Princess?" crowed the weather cock. Percy was too surprised to do anything but nod and the iron bird rattled into the air screaming: "The Princess! The Princess!" and flew over the tree tops.

CHAPTER 17

The Adventurers Meet

"I DON'T SEE any Princess," sniffed the old soldier, coming to an abrupt halt and eying the two travellers critically. Grampa and his army had barely recovered from their tumble off the rainbow before Bill's cries, announcing the Princess, brought them hurrying to the tulip tree, where Dorothy and Percy Vere were resting.

"Am I dreaming?" gulped the Forgetful Poet, clutching Dorothy's hand. "Am I dreaming or what?" His eye roved from Grampa's game leg

178

to Tatters' many-hued suit and finally came to a rest on the lovely little flower fairy.

"There is the Princess," insisted Bill, pointing his claw at Dorothy.

"Snuff and nonsense!" snapped the old soldier scornfully. "You're a regular false alarm, Bill, always going off at the wrong time. Why, that's only a dusty little country girl and no proper match for the Prince at all!"

Grampa's lofty speech brought Percy quickly out of his dream.

"Don't you be so migh and highty," muttered the Forgetful Poet, drawing himself up proudly. "You don't know what you're talking about, you—"

"No offense! No offense!" observed Grampa coolly. "It's not the child's fault that she's not a Princess. I dare say she's a very nice little girl, but we're looking for a Princess!"

"Why, so are we!" cried Dorothy in surprise. "But you needn't be so impolite."

"She is a Princess, too, and do you mean to stand there and tell me that that young ragbag is a Prince?" Percy Vere stared at Tatters long and earnestly and then, rolling up his eyes murmured feelingly:

> "A Prince of rags and scraps and patches,
> And then they talk to *us* of matches!
> The Prince of what? The Prince of where?
> He has a bird's nest in his—er in his—"

"Hair," giggled Dorothy. Poor Tatters

blushed to his ears and hurriedly tried to smooth out his hair with his fingers.

"Come on?" cried Grampa indignantly. "They're crazy!"

"If you'll believe he's a Prince, I'll believe she's a Princess," put in a soft voice and Urtha, who had been listening anxiously to the sharp speeches on both sides, danced up to the Forgetful Poet.

"That's fair enough," agreed Percy Vere, smiling at the little flower fairy:

"You believe in us, and we'll believe in you,
And if *you* say so I'll believe that six and one
   are—are—?"

"Two," said Dorothy, "only they're eight. You mustn't mind Percy's forgetting. You see, he is a poet," she explained hastily.

"Let me out! Let me out! What's all this noise?"

Dorothy and the Forgetful Poet exchanged frightened glances and Toto crept back of the tree-trunk with only one ear showing, for the voice certainly had come from a bag on the Prince's shoulder.

"Not a dream, but a night mare!" choked the Forgetful Poet, as the Prince of Ragbad calmly took his father's head out of the knitting bag and held it up toward them.

"Don't be alarmed," purred Fumbo in his drowsy voice, as the two clung to one another in a panic.

"I'm not alarmed, I'm—I'm petrified!" gasped Percy, looking over his shoulder to see whether the path was clear in case he should desire to run.

"It has a crown on," whispered Dorothy nervously. "It must be a King. I once knew a Princess who had dozens of heads and took them off. Maybe he's like that."

"You're speaking of the Princess Languidere, I presume," drawled Fumbo. Being a great reader, Fumbo was well acquainted with all the celebrities in Oz. "No, my dear, I am not like that; as it happens I have only one head and it blew off, as you can plainly see. This young man you see here is my son and he is carrying my head back to my body. And now you may tell me *your* story," commanded the King, smiling graciously. His glance rested curiously on Dorothy. "You are known to me already," continued the King. "Grampa, this is Princess Dorothy of Oz, and she is even prettier than her pictures, if you will permit me to say so."

"I told you she was a Princess," crowed the weather cock triumphantly. "Have you a fortune with you, girl?"

"The Dorothy who lives in the Emerald City?" gasped Tatters, almost dropping his father's head. "The Dorothy who discovered Oz?"

Dorothy nodded modestly and Grampa, covered with confusion at the memory of his sharp speech, tried to hide behind Tatters.

"Never mind," laughed Dorothy, seeing Grampa's embarrassment. "I really don't look like a Princess now. You see we've had such a hard journey, falling down a mountain and all, we're kinda rumpled."

"We've been through a week of wash-days," groaned Percy Vere, straightening his jacket and looking ruefully at his red hands. "I'm sorry I didn't realize you were a Prince." He turned contritely to Tatters. "Mistakes all around, you see."

"Well, we've had a hard time, too," admitted the Prince of Ragbad, making another frantic attempt to smooth his hair.

"Ask her if she has a fortune?" insisted Bill, settling heavily on the Prince's shoulder.

"Hush!" said Tatters, giving Bill a poke.

"Oh, goody! goody! We're all going to be friends." Urtha spread out her flowery skirts and danced happily around the little group. "Oh, forget-me-nots and daisies! Oh, dahlias and pinks!"

"And you're the whole bouquet, Miss May!" cried Percy Vere, but he was immediately interrupted by Fumbo.

"Stop!" cried the King's head. "Let us keep these stories straight. You said you were looking for a Princess. What Princess?"

"Company, sit down!" ordered the old soldier gruffly. He had commanded the expedition so far and was not going to be bossed around at this stage of the game. Tatters and Urtha promptly obeyed, the Prince carefully holding his father's head in his lap. Dorothy and Percy Vere, after their long run, were glad enough to rest. So down they all sat in a big circle under the green tree, Bill and Toto in the center, staring at one another curiously.

"Now, then, Mr er—Mr—" Grampa nodded condescendingly at the Forgetful Poet.

"Vere," put in Percy politely.

"Now then, Mr Vere, let us have your story," said the old soldier, taking a big pinch of snuff. So, with many interruptions from King Fumbo—who seemed to know all about Perhaps City—and many lapses into verse, the Forgetful Poet told of Abrog's prophecy about the monster, of the strange disappearance of the little Princess and Abrog himself, of his

183

tumble down Maybe Mountain and of his and Dorothy's adventures since then on the Runaway and Monday Mountain.

"Humph," grunted the old soldier, when he had finished, "I wouldn't trust a prophet as far as I could swing a chimney by the smoke. That prophet has run off with her. You can bet your last shoe button on that and, since we are searching for a Princess ourselves, we might as well look for the Princess of Perhaps City. What do you say, my boy?" Grampa glanced questioningly at Tatters.

"I'll be glad to help Princess Dorothy and this—this poet, but—." Already Tatters had made up his mind to return with Urtha to Ragbad, regardless of fortunes and Princesses.

"No buts about it," roared the King's head indignantly. "She'll be a splendid match for you, my son, and Peer Haps, from all reports, is one of the merriest monarchs in Oz. Why, I dote on him already!"

"Can't all this wait till we find the Princess?" protested Percy Vere nervously. "No use rushing matters, you know." All this talk of marrying rather upset him. Tatters looked gratefully at the Forgetful Poet and decided to forgive him for his rude verse.

"Of course it can wait," agreed the Prince heartily. "The first thing to do is to rescue the Princess."

"No, the first thing to do, is to tell us who

you are," laughed Dorothy, who could restrain her curiosity no longer. "Why, we don't even know your names or how you happened to be in this part of Oz."

"We followed the directions on the bottle," explained Bill importantly. "We fell, swum, exploded, sailed and flew!"

"You tell them," begged Tatters, looking appealingly at the old soldier, for he could see that Bill was going to mix things dreadfully.

"Yes, you tell us," commanded Fumbo. He had not yet heard the story of their journey from Ragbad himself, and was even more curious about it than Dorothy. So Grampa took the center of the circle. Now, next to fighting, the old soldier loved to talk and, next to fighting, talking was the best thing he did. His recital of the experiences of his little army during the past three days was so thrilling that Dorothy and Percy simply held their breath and Toto's ears waved with excitement. Dorothy was particularly interested in Bill and the strange manner in which he had been shocked to life. Being from the United States herself, it seemed real homelike to meet a fellow countryman, even if he was only a weather cock. As for Percy Vere—who had lived all his life on Maybe Mountain—nothing could exceed his astonishment as Grampa proceeded from one adventure to the next.

"Do you mind if I close my eyes," Percy

muttered weakly, as Grampa reached the point in his story where they had discovered Urtha growing in the wizard's garden. "Do you mind if I close my eyes? I can believe anything with my eyes shut."

"Not if you close your mouth also," snapped Grampa and went right on with his story, never even stopping for breath until he had reached their last tumble from the rainbow.

"Professor Wogglebug will have to write a whole new history," breathed Dorothy, as Grampa settled back in his place, "and Ozma will never allow the bandit to stay in the blue forest nor Gorba to practice magic in his hidden garden. Oh, my! I do believe you can help us find the Princess after all. You are so brave and interesting." Dorothy smiled at Grampa and Tatters and the Forgetful Poet, opening his eyes, stared dreamily at the little flower fairy.

"If I had my arms, I'd embrace you all," exclaimed Fumbo feelingly, "and you shall have hugs all around as soon as I get back to my body. You're a credit to the country, and Bill here shall have a perch on the highest tower in Ragbad and little Miss Posies—"

"But the Princess!" exclaimed Bill anxiously, "and the fortune! We can't go back without them!"

"Too late to hunt for them to-day," chuckled Grampa and indeed, while they had been talking, the sun had dropped down behind the daisy splashed hill, leaving the world bathed in a pleasant dusk.

"We're all tired, so we'll have supper and make camp here," decided Grampa sensibly. "Then tomorrow we'll start after that prophet with gun, musket, sword and bootleather!"

"That's the talk!" cried Percy Vere, jumping up to help Tatters gather wood for a fire. With such good company, the last of the bear steaks from Isa Poso and the berries gathered by little Urtha tasted better than a feast, and nothing could have exceeded the jollity of that evening 'round Grampa's camp fire.

Between the Forgetful Poet's verse and the old soldier's jokes, they were simply convulsed and finally, when they had talked over their adventures to heart's content, Dorothy, Tatters, the Forgetful Poet and Urtha settled down to a quiet game of scrum. Soon the only sound to be heard was the click of the checkers on Grampa's game leg and the loud snores of Fumbo's head, which hung from a branch of the tulip tree in the pink knitting bag of Maribella, the little sky shepherdess.

CHAPTER 18

The Mischievous Play Fellows

B RIGHT and early next morning Grampa lined up his little army and, after a short council, they determined to continue their march to the Emerald City and learn from Ozma's magic picture just where Abrog and the lost Princess of Perhaps City were to be found. Although breakfast had been a light affair of water and berries, they were all in excellent spirits and, with Grampa's drum beating out a lively march, they stepped merrily down the shady Winkie Lane. Grampa and the

Forgetful Poet led off, Dorothy and the Prince of Ragbad followed, the Prince carrying his father's head and his red umbrella. Urtha danced in and out to suit her own sweet fancy, Bill flew ahead and Toto trotted contentedly behind.

"Here I go by the name of Bill!" crowed the weather cock exultantly. "By the name of B-hill!"

Grampa winked at Percy Vere and Percy Vere winked back. "Isn't he ridiculish?" whispered the Forgetful Poet merrily. "But then, we're all ridiculish in spots." His eyes rested a moment on Grampa's game leg. "Yes," continued Percy Vere, with a droll nod, "everything, when you come to think of it, is simply sinoobious. Why do we call ourselves an army, pray, when we might just as well call ourselves a footy? Have we not as many feet as arms? Why do we say 'Good-day' on a rainy morning and—"

"One thing at a time, one thing at a time!" objected the old soldier testily. "Aren't you afraid you'll strain your brain, young man?"

"I think and think both late and early,
For thinking makes the brain grow curly!"

chuckled the irrepressible poet, at which Grampa beat such a tattoo upon his drum that the next verses were quite drowned out. But as soon as Grampa stopped drumming, Percy burst out again:

The Mischievous Play Fellows

"I met a spick and Spaniard once,
He was so spick and span,
He even had his toes curled up
Believe me, if you, if you—?"

"I can believe anything Mr Vere," said
Grampa grimly.

"Then try this!" roared the Forgetful Poet,
waving his arms.

"If fifty boats and fifty crews
Were gathered in a group,
Why wouldn't it be proper, Sir,
To call the crews a croup?
Admit, old dear, that this is clear—
As clear, as clear as—"

"Soup!" groaned Grampa in spite of himself.
"Vegetable soup," he added bitterly and, reaching in his pocket, jerked out the wizard's
medicine.

"What are you doing?" asked Percy curiously,
as he ran his finger hurriedly down the green
label.

"Looking for a cure," said the old sailor,
raising his eyebrows significantly. But there
was no cure for forgetful poetry on the green
label, so with a sigh Grampa returned the
bottle to his pocket. "What can't be cured must
be endured," said the old soldier glumly and,
pursing up his lips, he began to whistle a sad
tune. Dorothy and Tatters exchanged amused
glances and Urtha, who had been skipping
beside Percy Vere, touched him on the arm.

"Is the Princess of Perhaps City pretty?" asked the little flower fairy timidly. She could not bear to think of Tatters marrying an ugly Princess.

"I should guess, mercy yes!
I should say, April, April—?"

"Trouble ahead! Trouble ahead!" crowed Bill, before anyone could finish the verse. Just then a turn in the lane brought them plump into a huge fenced-in park. The fence was much too high to climb and stretched as far on either side as they could see.

"I never saw this place before," said Dorothy, peering curiously between the bars, "but maybe if we knock on the gate someone will let us in. Then we can march through and out the other side."

"Here's the gate," called Percy Vere, who had run a little ways to the right, "and here's a sign."

"Play!" announced the sign over the gate. "All work on these grounds forbidden." Just below was a smaller sign—"No trespassing!"

"Well, we don't want to trespass, we want to jes' pass through," chortled the Forgetful Poet and, before anyone could stop him, he had hammered hard upon the gates. Immediately loud roars of laughter sounded all through the park, footsteps scurried over the lawns and the next instant the gayest company that

Dorothy ever had seen came crowding forward—Pierretttes and Pierrots, hundreds of
them, the girls in full skirted frocks with tall
saucy caps, the men in pantaloon suits and
frills. While they smiled and waved through
the bars, the King of Play, who looked, as
Dorothy told Ozma afterwards, exactly like a
court jester—the King himself swung open the
gates and, with a low bow, invited them to
enter. So, of course they did, and before
Grampa could give the order to break ranks or
fall out, or even say Hello, the Play Fellows
had fallen upon his army and simply borne
them away. Only Bill escaped and nervously he
hovered over his friends, determining, if necessary, to drop on the heads of this exuberant
company.

"Wait! Stop! Halt!" puffed the old soldier,
who was being dragged toward a merry-go-
round by five of the mischievous Pierrettes.
Dorothy and Percy Vere were being rushed as
unceremoniously to the swings, while a dozen
of the Pierrots were begging Urtha for a dance.
Tatters, holding his father's head high above
his own, was hustled off to a high wooden slide
and to nothing that any of them said would the
Play Fellows pay the slightest attention. Indeed,
there was so much noise and confusion,
they could not have heard if they had tried.
Bands played and fountains played and the
Play Fellows played, and the creak of the
swings and the squeak of the merry-go-

rounds and the roars of the delighted Pierrettes and Pierrots, as they hustled their visitors from one amusement to another, were enough to deafen a gate post. Toto, after one shocked glance at the boisterous company, scampered off and hid himself in a button bush, where he watched anxiously for a chance to escape. Poor Bill, trying to keep all of the company in view at once, flew in dizzying circles over the park, almost cross-eyed from the strain.

After his sixteenth merry-go-round, Grampa gave up trying to explain and, staggering over to a soap bubble fountain, fell in. But the Play Fellows quickly pulled him out and insisted upon his joining in a game of tag. The only bright spot in the whole dreadful experience was the finding of a bubble pipe, which Grampa hastily picked from its bush and thrust into his pocket.

Percy and Dorothy fared no better. "This is worse than washing!" groaned the Forgetful Poet, as a wild company of Pierrettes dragged them 'round and 'round the mulberry bush.

"Play! Play! Play!" shouted King Capers, dashing from group to group and banging the company right and left with his belled and beribboned scepter. "Play! Play! Play!"

"I never knew fun was such hard work," panted Tatters to Bill, who was circling immediately above his head. The poor Prince was black and blue all over from sliding down the slides, but every time he objected the Play

Fellows would pull him to the top and scream with merriment as he came sliding down again. There were too many heads to fall on, and Bill—powerless to help—screamed his rage and indignation at the mannerless crowd. There was much to be seen and marvelled at in the play grounds, but as the company agreed later, playing when you want to play and being forced to play are two quite different things, so that the balloon vines, top trees and checker bushes went almost unnoticed. Indeed all that any of them could think of was getting away.

Urtha was the first to make her escape. The little flower fairy had been treated so gently and considerately by Grampa and Tatters, since her coming to life in the enchanted garden, that she did not know what to make of the rude manners of the Play Fellows. When they

began snatching flowers from her hair and pulling her roughly from place to place, her violet eyes widened with terror and dismay. Watching her opportunity, she sprang away from them and sped like the wind itself across the gardens. Now the runner does not exist who can outdistance a fairy, so it was not long before Urtha left her tormentors behind. And better still, the little flower fairy had run directly into a wicket gate leading out of the play grounds. Opening the gate she slipped through and then, because she was still frightened, she kept running and running till she was as lost as one raindrop in a thunder shower.

There is no telling how long the others would have been forced to endure the teasing of the Play Fellows, if a gong had not sounded from a distant part of the grounds. Immediately the whole company trooped off and, without waiting to find out the meaning of the bell, Grampa's army rushed to the nearest exits.

"I'm done for!" gasped Percy Vere, rolling under a tree. "Let me curl up like a pretzel and bake—I mean die!" Toto, who had followed close upon the heels of the harassed company, curled up beside him.

"But where's Urtha?" cried Tatters, staring around wildly. "Where's Grampa?"

"She ran away long ago," crowed Bill, flying over the fence. "That way!" He pointed his claw toward the East.

"Oh, dear! Oh, dear, where *is* the old soldier?" wailed Dorothy, jumping up and down with impatience. "We ought to get away from here quick."

"I'll find him," volunteered Bill. "Wait here." Back went the devoted weather cock and, after flying over the entire play grounds, he found Grampa asleep under a checker bush.

"Wake up!" cried Bill, jumping up and down on his chest. "The coast is clear. Forward march, by the name of Grampa!"

The old soldier stirred uneasily, rubbed his eyes and then sprang up but immediately tumbled down again, for while he slept, the wretched Play Fellows had run off with his game leg.

"What in time?" blustered the old soldier,

picking himself up again. But being a man of action and, seeing a crowd of Pierrettes emerging from a big hall not far away, Grampa snatched up a long handled croquet mallet and, using it as a crutch, hobbled with all his might toward the exit pointed out by Bill. Here he was met by Percy Vere and Dorothy and after a startled look each seized one of his arms and away they ran as fast as five legs would take them. Percy carried the King's head and Dorothy the red umbrella. Tatters had dropped both when he discovered that Urtha was missing and had dashed off in search of her. And it was not long before he picked up the trail, for every step of the flower maiden was marked out in daisies and forget-me-nots. Paying no attention to rocks, sticks, brambles and thorns, the Prince of Ragbad pushed on, his only thought to find and comfort the sweet and lost little fairy who had made the days so pleasant and the journey so happy for them.

CHAPTER 19

Back to Perhaps City

SEATED on a great gold cushion on the lowest golden step of his palace sat Peer Haps, pointing his telescope with trembling fingers down Maybe Mountain. It was the fourth day mentioned in Abrog's prophecy, the day the monster was to carry off the Princess, and still no word had come from the Forgetful Poet. Between grief over the loss of his daughter and worry over Percy Vere, the poor old monarch had got no sleep at all and was so cross and snappy that the pages and courtiers went steathily about on tip-toe, their fingers to their lips.

"Can't you make a verse, idiot?" roared the Peer, glaring at Perix who, with another telescope, sat close beside him. Perix moved up a couple of steps and sadly shook his head.

"But look," he stuttered in the next breath, "someone is coming up the mountain."

"Is it the monster?" puffed Peer Haps anxiously. "Has it two heads?" Dropping his own telescope, he snatched the young noble-man's glass and glued his eye to the top. Then, with a loud shriek of joy, he tore open the gates and plunged recklessly down the steep mountain side. And certainly the dear old fellow would have rolled to the bottom had not a sturdy oak intervened and put a stop to his plunging. It was the fortunatest place of all for a stop, because, right below the oak, climbing easily over the rocks and stones, was the lost Princess herself. Not quite herself, perhaps, but enough so for her father to recognize her. Holding tight to the oak, the old Peer leaned down and seized her hand. The next instant he had her in his arms and was running up the mountain as recklessly as he had just plunged down. But some good fairy kept him from tumbling and, once up the golden steps, he brushed past gaping courtiers and pages and never stopped till he had reached the great throne room.

Setting the Princess on a green satin sofa, he gave her a hasty kiss and, without stopping to question her about her strange disappearance, locked the door and rushed from the room. Beads of perspiration stood out on his forehead. True, the Princess was found, but she certainly was changed and, worse still, at any moment the monster might appear and carry her off. Thudding down the corridor, Peer Haps burst into the apartment of the tall High Humpus of Perhaps City. Humpus was also Chief Justice and attended to all state weddings. The Peer was determined to have the Princess marry Petrix at once and settle this monster matter once and for always. Explaining this as he went along, he dragged the scandalized Justice to the steps to fetch the groom. But Perix had disappeared and with him every single young and single nobleman in Perhaps City. For though Peer Haps had run quickly, with his daughter in his arms, he had not run quickly enough, and word of the mysterious change in the Princess had already spread over the city.

"She is bewitched," Perix had whispered to the others in a panic and—feeling in his bones that Peer Haps would insist upon marrying her anyway—the faint-hearted youth had hidden himself in a rain barrel and the other young noblemen, equally alarmed, had run to the darkest cellar in the castle. Hopping on one foot and then on the other, Peer Haps called each one by name. But there was no response and, sinking down upon the golden steps, the poor King wept with rage and discouragement.

But the Lord High Humpus had been staring down the mountain for signs of the monster, and now he plucked the Peer sharply by the sleeve.

"Look!" hissed the Chief Justice, every curl in his white wig fluttering with excitement. "Look!" Knocking upon the great gates of the city was a weary, travel-stained young stranger. It was the Prince of Ragbad. For the flower trail had led him straight to the foot of Maybe Mountain. There he had lost his way, for Maybe Mountain is covered with wild flowers of every description, so that it was impossible to trace farther the footsteps of the little fairy. But Tatters had kept on, nevertheless, determined, if necessary, to search the whole mountain until he found her. Naturally, he did not know he was so near the Forgetful Poet's old home. But when, after a hard climb he reached the mountain top and spied the splendid castle of Peer Haps, he decided to continue his search there and waited impatiently for someone to open the gates.

"He looks honest," sputtered the Chief Justice, raising his brows significantly, "and in spite of his rags he is not unhandsome. Suppose—"

To the rest of the sentence Peer Haps paid no attention, for he had already flung down the steps and pulled Tatters through the gates. Grabbing him by the arm, he hurried him up the steps and along the hall before the startled Prince could say "Jack Robinson." The Lord High Humpus, straightening his wig, had dashed after them, and, while Peer Haps unlocked the door of the throne room, he held Tatters tightly by the hand.

"What's the matter?" demanded the astonished youth. He was exhausted and out of breath from his scramble up the mountain. "What's the matter? I am looking for a lost fairy. Have you seen anything of her?" But instead of answering, the Chief Justice put his fingers to his lips and drew the young man into the throne room itself. There was a confused mumble of words, to which Tatters, who still was too weary and breathless to argue, paid small attention. He nodded absently to some question of the white-wigged dignitary and the next minute was being crushed in the embrace of the singularly fat old gentleman who had dragged him up the steps.

"You have saved us!" cried Peer Haps, tears of joy zig-zagging down his cheek. "My son! My son! How can I ever repay you!"

"Son?" The Prince of Ragbad sprang back aghast.

"Congratulations!" chuckled the Chief Justice, clapping Tatters on the back.

"On what?" gasped the bewildered young Prince, whirling 'round.

"On your marriage." The Chief Justice made a deep bow toward the cloaked figure, whom Tatters had not seen until now.

"My marriage?" The distracted youth clapped one hand to his head and the other to his heart and fell backwards upon a page who had just run in to announce visitors. But before the

page could announce them, Grampa, Percy Vere, Dorothy and Toto burst into the throne room. It had not been long before they, too, had picked up the flower trail of Urtha and later the footprints of Tatters himself. You can imagine the delight of the Forgetful Poet to find himself once more on familiar ground. It was a hard pull up, for the old soldier had but one leg to climb with, but they had finally reached the top of the mountain, and, waving aside courtiers and servants, they had hurried immediately to the throne room.

"Have you seen anything of a little fairy?" puffed all three together, and then seeing Tatters, apparently having a fit in the arms of a page, they stopped short.

"Why, Tatters, whatever's the matter?" Dorothy dropped the red umbrella and ran over to the Prince of Ragbad.

"Matter?" choked the poor Prince, tears streaming down his cheeks. "Matter! I'm married to I don't know whom—that's what's the matter!" And before Dorothy could make head or tail of his story the Forgetful Poet and Peer Haps had rushed at each other with such an outpouring of affectionate greetings, such hugs and claps upon the back, that nothing else could be heard at all.

"This is worse than a battle," groaned the old soldier, bracing himself against the table.

"It's an outrage, an utter outrage. Pick me up! Pick me up! Do you hear?" The wig of the

Chief Justice rose into the air and turned round three times. The voice had certainly come from a pink bag at his feet, for the Forgetful Poet, in his excitement at seeing the old Peer, had carelessly dropped Fumbo's head. Pale with

terror, the High Humpus fled from the throne room, and it was just as well, for there was noise and confusion enough without him. As no one else heard Fumbo, he had to stay where he was.

"But the Princess!" cried Percy Vere, extricating himself at last from the Peer's embraces. "I could not find her, but all these people are going to help and—"

"Don't worry about that," beamed Peer Haps, waving toward the quiet little figure. "She is not only found, but married. Now let the monster appear if he dare. This young man has saved the day."

"Do you mean to say you are married?" roared Grampa, thumping on the table with his fist and glaring over at Tatters. "Why didn't you wait for us? Where's Urtha? Where's the Princess? Why is she all covered up like this? I insist upon seeing the Princess."

"One minute! One minute!" begged Peer Haps, stepping between Grampa and the cloaked figure. "My daughter is bewitched just now and cannot be seen, but I'm sure the spell can be broken, and then—"

"And you've married a bewitched Princess?" With another angry glance at poor Tatters, Grampa bit off a piece of his bubble pipe and sank heavily into a pink armchair. Dorothy had been trying her best to unravel the strange mix-up and now stepped forward.

"Let Tatters tell what happened," said the little Princess, stamping her foot imperiously. "It wasn't his fault, Grampa." She spoke with such firmness that Peer Haps fairly gasped. Then, stealing a second glance and recognizing her instantly as a Princess Royal of Oz, he motioned for Tatters to speak.

So the Prince of Ragbad rose up and in breathless sentences explained how he had been seized at the gates of the city and tricked into marrying the Princess.

"But isn't that what you were going to do anyway?" asked Percy Vere, when the Prince

207

had finished. "Weren't you looking for a Princess and a fortune when I met you? And didn't we all decide to hunt the Princess of Perhaps City? Well! Here she is—and there you are! The only difference is that you have married her a little sooner than you intended and saved her from an unknown and dreadful monster. Nothing so terrible about that. My hat!" Percy Vere smiled coaxingly at the Prince and encouragingly at Peer Haps, for he did not like to see any of his friends unhappy.

"But I was only going to rrr-rescue her," wailed Tatters.

"The difference is that we haven't seen the Princess," put in Grampa more mildly. "We'd save anybody from a monster, but don't you think, Mr Vere, it was unfair to marry Tatters to a Princess he's never even seen?"

"Idiot," screamed a harsh voice. Whirling around, the startled company saw a bent and dreadful old man standing just inside the long window. "Idiot!" he shrieked again, pointing a long trembling finger at Peer Haps. "You have married your daughter to a monster!"

"It's Abrog," gasped Percy Vere, clutching Dorothy's hand.

"Monster," roared Grampa, and hopping over to the Prophet, he seized him by the beard. "How dare you call Tatters a monster? I'll fight you!" puffed the old soldier furiously.

Jerking away, Abrog leaned down, picked up

208

209

Fumbo's head and set it upon Tatters' shoulders. "See," he screamed wildly, "you have married your daughter to a monster with two heads." And as Peer Haps, who knew nothing of Tatters' story, fell back aghast, Fumbo stuck his head out of the bag and began scolding everyone in the room.

In the uproar that followed and while Percy, Dorothy, and Grampa were trying all at once to explain things to the old Peer, the Prophet himself began to move stealthily toward the Princess. Only Tatters saw this. Placing his

father's head carefully on the table, he reached out and, just as Abrog reached her, the Prince seized him roughly by the collar. But he was not quick enough. Abrog had already snatched away the cloak and there—trembling and sorrowful—stood the Princess of Perhaps City, herself. Tatters loosed his hold upon the Prophet.

"Urtha," cried the overwrought young bridegroom and took the frightened little fairy in his arms.

CHAPTER 20

The Prophet Confesses

YOU can well imagine the surprise of Grampa and his little army to discover that the flower maiden whom they had been loving all this while was really the lost Princess. How the story ever would have been straightened out had it not been for Dorothy, I have no idea.

"Why didn't you tell us it was Urtha?" shouted Grampa, shaking his finger indignantly at Peer Haps.

"And who is Urtha?" gasped the astonished

old monarch, fanning himself with his crown, for he was in such a state by this time that he hardly knew what he was doing. "My daughter's name is Pretty Good—isn't it, my dear?"

The little flower fairy shook her head solemnly. "My name is Urtha," she insisted softly. "Isn't it, Tatters?"

"She's bewitched," groaned the King.

"She's bewitching," corrected Grampa.

"Stop! Stop!" said Dorothy. "We'll never get things straightened out this way. Everybody sit down and—quick—quick—catch that Prophet!" Abrog had been slyly edging toward the door, but the Forgetful Poet, with a quick bound, brought him back.

"Now then," said Dorothy, when they were all seated, "I believe Abrog is at the bottom of the whole business. Let's make him tell. Did you bewitch this Princess?" she demanded sternly.

Abrog only mumbled and scowled and refused to speak a word. "Better answer this young lady," puffed Peer Haps warningly. "She is a Princess of Oz, and can have you well punished."

"Speak up, you old villain!" shouted Grampa, waving his sword over the Prophet's head. But Abrog stood still and stubbornly refused to say a word, until the old soldier suddenly bethought himself of the wizard's medicine. "Maybe there's a cure for the tongue tied on this," muttered Grampa. Taking out the bottle, he began to scan the green label. At the first sight of the medicine, a dreadful change came over the Prophet. He turned a sickly green and began to tremble violently.

"Give me that bottle! Give me that bottle, and I will tell all," he panted, trying desperately to snatch it from Grampa.

"Don't you do it," cried the Prince of Ragbad. "Why, Grampa, I believe—I believe this is the wizard himself."

"But it says 'Gorba,' " muttered the old soldier, holding the bottle high above his head. "Don't you remember?"

"Gorba!" exclaimed Dorothy, writing the word with her finger in the air. "Why G-o-r-b-a is A-b-r-o-g spelled backwards!"

"Abrog and Gorba!" shrieked Percy Vere, bounding to his feet. The poet instantly broke into verse in his customary style:

"Abrog and Gorba are one and the same—
A prophet and wizard wrapped up in one—
    one—one?"

"Name!" finished Peer Haps, almost tumbling from his throne.

"This is the most exciting story I ever was in," wheezed the head of Fumbo, from its place on the table. The Prophet had fairly crumpled up at Dorothy's discovery and, seeing that further resistance was useless, he whined out the whole of his story. Determined to save

214

Pretty Good from the monster and marry her himself, he had decided to change her to mud. For a Princess as ugly as mud, even a monster would not marry, explained the old villain tearfully. So for this purpose he had carried her to the hidden garden, where all his magic appliances were kept. But so sweet, lovely and good was the little Princess of Perhaps City, that the evil spell of the wizard, instead of changing her to a muddy image as Abrog intended, had turned her into a bewitching little flower fairy. Disappointed at the way his magic had worked, Abrog had nevertheless resolved to keep her under the spell until after the day of the prophecy and then change her back to her own self and marry her at once. But when he returned to the garden he found her gone and he had hurried as fast as he could back to Perhaps City. How he had been robbed of his magic medicine on the first day he bewitched Urtha, and how Urtha herself had been released by Tatters and Grampa, we know.

"But what about this monster?" panted the old soldier, as Abrog finished speaking and began uncomfortably shuffling his feet on the golden floor.

"Let me see that prophecy," demanded Dorothy. The unwilling Prophet drew the crumpled parchment from his sleeve.

"A youth, wrapped in the skin of an old bear—a youth with two heads upon his shoulders and carrying a red umbrella—will marry the Princess of Perhaps City," read Dorothy in some surprise.

"Why, that's Tatters!" cried the little girl in delight.

"Of course it is," declared Grampa. "Why, there isn't any monster at all. Whoever said there was?" He stared around triumphantly and Peer Haps pointed angrily at the old Prophet, who was hopping about in a vain attempt to escape.

"What shall we do to him?" asked the Forgetful Poet, seizing Abrog by the collar and holding him, kicking and struggling, in the air. Some said this and some said that, but it was Grampa, running his finger quickly down the trusty green label, who finally decided the matter. For listed under sorcery he found a sure cure for Abrog.

"Break a saucer of the mixture over the sorcerer's head," directed the bottle severely. So a saucer was quickly brought and, paying no attention to the squalls and screams of the scheming old Prophet, Grampa broke it over his head. At the first crack of the china, Abrog disappeared and, as every one jumped with surprise, a little brown mouse scurried across the room.

"Well, he won't do much harm in that shape," sighed Grampa, as Toto went sniffing all around the throne under which the mouse had disappeared.

"But my daughter!" cried Peer Haps sud-

denly. "Who will unbewitch the Princess now?"
The company exchanged dismayed glances,
realizing too late that they should have forced
Abrog to disenchant Urtha before they punished
him.

CHAPTER 21

Urtha Is Transformed

YOU are probably wondering why Urtha herself had stood so silently during all the commotion in the castle. Well, in the first place the little flower fairy was so frightened by her experiences with the Play Fellows that her only thought had been of escape. With the Prophet's spell had gone all memory of her former existence as Princess of Perhaps City and when Peer Haps had found her on Maybe Mountain and hurried her back to the castle she was more frightened still. Not knowing

218

where she was, nor what to do, the confused little fairy had done nothing at all. Trembling under the big cloak, she had stood and waited for something terrible to happen and when at last she did hear the familiar voices of Tatters and Grampa and thought they were angry at her, she trembled more than ever and was afraid to speak or move at all. But now that the mystery was about cleared up, Urtha was so happy just to be with the Prince of Ragbad again that she paid small attention to the excitement about her enchantment. Neither did Tatters, for the lovely little flower fairy suited him exactly as she was. While they were whispering cozily about Ragbad and other terribly important matters, Dorothy and Grampa got their heads together and solved the last of the adventurers' problems. For Dorothy, bending excitedly over Grampa's shoulder, discovered a cure for enchantment on the wizard's bottle. "Three drops on the head," advised the green label. Grampa squinted anxiously into the bottle, for he had poured nearly the whole contents over Abrog.

"Is there enough?" whispered Dorothy. Grampa, shaking his head doubtfully, tip-toed over to Urtha and, while Percy Vere, Peer Haps and Dorothy watched with breathless interest, he shook the bottle over her head. One drop! Two drops! And—after a violent shake—three fell upon the soft fern hair of the littler fairy. As the third drop fell the little flower girl melted away before their eyes into a rainbow mist of lovely colors. Out of the mist stepped a no less lovely Princess—a Princess so like Urtha that Grampa blinked and Tatters could hardly believe his senses. Though no longer a little lady of flowers, Urtha still carried the flowers' lovely colors and the flowers' lovely fragrance in her exquisite little person. Violets were no bluer than Urtha's eyes; roses never pinker than Urtha's cheeks; apple blossoms no fairer than Urtha's skin.

Trembling with relief and happiness, Peer Haps clasped her in his arms and, with the little Princess on his knee, insisted on hearing every word of the long, strange story. And about time it was that he did, for all this while he had been trying to explain to himself the presence of Fumbo's head. But when Grampa had told their adventures from beginning to end, Peer Haps welcomed the King of Ragbad as heartily as if his whole body were present, and they all sat down to talk things over.

Just as Grampa was telling again exactly how they had discovered Urtha, there was a loud screech in the corridor, and in flew the brave weather cock, whom no one had missed in the terrible commotion.

"Here I come by the name of Bill," crowed the excited bird and flying over to Grampa, he proudly dropped Grampa's lost leg into his lap. For while the others had hurried up the mountain Bill had flown back to the playground

and snatched Grampa's leg away from King Capers and two of the mischievous Pierrettes who were deeply engrossed in the game of scrum. It had taken Bill some time but here at last he was and, joyfully buckling on his leg, Gramps danced a jig on the spot. For now his happiness was complete—Peer Haps having already given him a pipe. Everyone made such a fuss over Bill that he felt fully repaid for his trouble.

Indeed, it was hard to tell who, of all that merry company, was the merriest—the Forgetful Poet at finding himself safely home, Peer Haps at finding his daughter, Grampa at the recovery of his leg, Urtha and Tatters or Dorothy and Toto at the splendid way the adventure had turned out.

Chuckling with delight, Peer Haps ran off

to fetch his yellow hen, for he was determined that Tatters should have the fortune—a reward of a thousand gold bricks.

"Is that the fortune?" asked Bill indignantly, as he placed the yellow hen in Tatters' arms. "Why, it's nothing but a bunch of feathers!"

"Don't you crow over me," screeched the yellow hen and, flying up, she laid a gold brick upon the table, much to the astonishment of Bill and the delight of the others.

While they still were laughing there was a blinding flash, and the yellow hen, Bill, Toto, Peer Haps and every other single person in the throne room disappeared. Yes, sir, they were gone—as gone as a box of last year's Christmas candy.

CHAPTER 22
Rejoicing in Ragbad

GONE, you say. But where? I might as well tell you at once that they were gone from Perhaps City because they already were in Ragbad standing in a surprised group in the shabby ballroom of the red castle. For Ozma, looking that morning in the magic picture to see why Dorothy had not returned to the Emerald City, had seen the little girl and her companions and all day had been following their adventures.

With the aid of a powerful radio belonging to the Wizard of Oz, she had heard the whole story Grampa had just related and determined, by her magic belt, to send them all safely home.

"They've had enough adventures," smiled this wise little ruler, and because she knew Dorothy, the Forgetful Poet and Peer Haps would want to meet Mrs Sew-and-Sew and the rest of Tatters' friends, she had sent them along too. But, best of all, she had, aided by the wizard's magic, wished Fumbo's head firmly and permanently back upon his body. When Pudge and Mrs Sew-and-Sew, aroused by all the confusion, came running to see what was the matter, imagine their surprise to find Fumbo in full possession of his head, welcoming Peer Haps, Dorothy and the Forgetful Poet to Ragbad.

And now what a flurry of introductions and explanations, what hugs, kisses and congratulations all 'round! Mrs Sew-and-Sew could hardly believe her good fortune and had to kiss Tatters every few minutes to see if he really were there and Urtha every few minutes to see if she really were true. After she had heard the whole story from beginning to end, she sent Pudge off to summon the twenty-four rustic laborers and rushed off to prepare such a feast as the old red castle had not known since her own wedding day—a feast with six kinds of ice cream and seven kinds of cake and two helpings of turkey for everyone. Far into the night the merrymaking lasted, for after the feast itself the old soldier insisted that they dance the Ragbad Quadrille.

"Oh, let's!" cried the Princess, remembering

how she and Tatters had danced upon the iceberg. So lines were quickly formed on each side of the ballroom.

"Come along, monster!" cried Urtha, leading off merrily with the Prince, as Grampa burst into the spirited music of the dance. Mrs Sew-and-Sew and Peer Haps came next, then the Forgetful Poet and Dorothy, then Fumbo and Pudge, the twenty-four rustic laborers filling in as they were needed. Not until the loud crows of Bill announced the rising of the sun did the party break up, and only then after a hundred rousing cheers had been given for the Prince and Princess of Ragbad. After luncheon next day, Dorothy and Toto, Peer Haps and the Forgetful Poet were magically transported back home by thoughtful little Ozma but, before she left, Dorothy made them promise to visit her in the Emerald City and I have no doubt that they will.

When Dorothy reached home the first person to greet her was her old friend, the Tin Woodman, smiling as he always smiles.

From that day on, let me say, Ragbad was a changed Kingdom for, as the twenty-four rustic laborers sold the gold bricks as fast as they were laid by the yellow hen, there was plenty of money to buy supplies and care for the linens and lawns. Grampa and Tatters had record crops and soon everything was so prosperous that Mrs Sew-and-Sew took off her thimble,

put on her crown and became Queen of Ragbad again.

As for Tatters and Urtha, the last I heard of them, they were happy as the days were long—as happy as only the dear folk in Oz know how to be. So that is all of the story of the Princess who was once a fairy, the poet who forgot his words, the old soldier who was always a hero and the Prince who went in search of his father's head.

THE INTERNATIONAL WIZARD OF OZ CLUB

The International Wizard of Oz Club was founded in 1957 to bring together all those interested in Oz, its authors and illustrators, film and stage adaptations, toys and games, and associated memorabilia. From a charter group of 16, the club has grown until today it has over 1800 members of all ages throughout the world. Its magazine, *The Baum Bugle*, first appeared in June 1957 and has been published continuously ever since. The *Bugle* appears three times a year and specializes in popular and scholarly articles about Oz and its creators, biographical and critical studies, first edition checklists, research into the people and places within the Oz books, etc. The magazine is illustrated with rare photographs and drawings, and the covers are in full color. The Oz Club also publishes a number of other Oz-associated items, including full-color maps; an annual collection of original Oz stories; books; and essays.

Each year, the Oz Club sponsors conventions in different areas of the United States. These gatherings feature displays of rare Oz and Baum material, an Oz quiz, showings of Oz films, an auction of hard-to-find Baum and Oz items, much conversation about Oz in all its aspects, and many other activities.

The International Wizard of Oz Club appeals to the serious student and collector of Oz as well as to any reader interested in America's own fairyland. For further information, please send a *long* self-addressed stamped envelope to:

Fred M. Meyer, Executive Secretary
THE INTERNATIONAL WIZARD
   OF OZ CLUB
Box 95
Kinderhook, IL 62345